I0586831

HEATHER BOYD

Never a Gentleman

HUNT CLUB – 5

DEDICATION

For Janette.

Your kind words obliterated a dark day and continue to lift my spirits even now. Thank you for keeping me writing and for being in my corner.

By Heather Boyd

Almost an Equal
Barely a Master
Hardly a Stranger

Just a Dream
Never a Gentleman
Once a Husband

CHAPTER ONE

Peace and quiet and no distractions made banker Victor Knight a very happy man. He flipped the page over, made note of expected expenses of his latest investment opportunity, then patted himself on the back for finding this gem among the detritus. At this rate, he'd be done with his calculations and home before night fell. Could his life be get any better?

"May I join you, Mr. Knight?"

Victor glanced up from his business papers and blinked at the Earl of Beecroft, where he hovered beside his table in the quiet dining room of the Hunt Club. The corner of the man's mouth curved upward as he stared. They'd had little to do with each other in past years, mostly because the earl came and went from Town rather frequently. They had spent an hour or more together earlier that day at Lord Norwich's residence though they had not spoken at the time. Which now seemed odd to Victor and perhaps a touch rude.

Determined to be more agreeable, Victor returned his scattered papers to the folio he carried, set them behind his back on the chair to keep the contents confidential, and smiled up at the man. "Yes, of course. By all means join me."

Lord Beecroft took the chair opposite, leaned back while a footman set a heaped plate before him. "I am much obliged to you," he murmured. "I can't stand sitting at a table alone when there is good company begging for more." He then dug in without another word.

Victor glanced at his neglected plate with little enthusiasm. More than likely the meal was cold, but he made himself eat a little more just to be polite. Between slow mouthfuls, Victor studied Beecroft openly. The earl was tall and broad in the chest, rather well known about Town, and extremely easy on the eye. His dark hair curled up at his collar, a little longer than was fashionable and his clothing was first rate. He was a man of means, a heavy signet ring on his right hand and gold pocket watch fob chain gleaming brightly at his waist, but he was not at all showy like some of his class.

"A devilishly tricky business today," Lord Beecroft muttered.

Victor glanced around them discreetly to see who might linger nearby. There was only Marcus Bright, Viscount Hambly, in sight but he was too far away to overhear this conversation. Victor hoped he kept his distance. The matter Lord Beecroft referred to had concerned the health of a Hunt Club member and thus required absolute discretion and the absence of harmful speculation on his part. Victor wasn't about to indulge in idle gossip when it concerned the succession of both titleholder and heir of the Norwich estate. He'd been present as a witness only, as a surety that no further harm would come to father and son. He'd not been asked to do more than that small favor. "It was."

He picked at a few of his favorite tidbits in silence, casting the odd glance at Lord Beecroft when he said nothing more on the matter. Victor had endured his fair share of odd exchanges with titled lords over the years, and he was strangely comforted by Beecroft's silence. As Beecroft finished his meal, he called over a footman. The earl requested their glasses be refilled with claret and he sat back with a contented sigh as if he planned to stay awhile. "Lovely weather we are having lately."

"Very warm indeed for this time of year," Victor replied as he reached for his refreshed glass and sipped. "I cannot remember it being so warm in September."

Lord Beecroft blue eyes creased at the corners as he smiled and the affect on Victor's senses was immediate. It struck him suddenly that it had been ages since he'd kissed a man. "I should have begun with the weather," Beecroft mused. "But usually that just makes me sound daft instead of impressing my companion."

Victor's face heated though he did his best to ignore it. "Why would you wish to impress me?"

"The better question is to ask why wouldn't I?" Lord Beecroft pushed his plate aside, a wry smile twisting his lips. He leaned forward across the table, a devilish warmth lighting his eyes, and slowly stroked one finger against the back of Victor's hand. "Do you know it's been rather difficult to catch your notice?"

Victor winced. His preoccupation with work had turned many a lover toward another when he didn't pay them enough attention. It wasn't that he was cold or indifferent. He just lacked the ability to balance a love life and work life to anyone else's satisfaction. He may as well be honest with Lord Beecroft before this conversation went any further. "I have heard that complaint before."

"Not a complaint. Every man has his own priorities. I admire dedication, Mr. Knight. You work long and diligent hours at your bank, but since subtlety hasn't worked in the past I'll be direct." He caught Victor's hand and held it. "I'd like to invite you to play."

Beecroft's hand was warm and surprisingly rough for a well-to-do lord.

"Play?" It took a moment to gather his wits largely because he was unused to being touched by a man in public. When he understood what he was being offered, his cock stirred to life. A night with Lord Beecroft's arms around him was unexpected. "Oh."

"Yes, *oh*." Lord Beecroft's gaze narrowed, focused directly on his face. His brow rose and he sat back, his touch sliding away. "Care to spend a few hours in bed with me?"

Victor had never been propositioned so directly before and he had to admit he was tempted. He wasn't the most popular of fellows. He was too serious, and as Lord Beecroft had mentioned, rather absorbed in his work at all hours of the day and night.

He studied Lord Beecroft carefully but could detect no trace of hesitation in his invitation. His smile was open and friendly and that appealed. The man wanted him and quite frankly, now that he was faced with the opportunity, Victor had to admit he wouldn't mind being tumbled. His collection of dildos and plugs might do for the odd night, but of late they lost their allure. Why not? Lord Beecroft had asked nicely. He nodded. "I'd love to."

"Excellent. I promise you will enjoy my company." Lord Beecroft clapped his hands and jumped to his feet as if on a spring. "I'll see Marinari about a room and meet you upstairs. Yes?"

"Yes." Victor was rather surprised by Beecroft's obvious enthusiasm for bed sport. It made him feel rather more desirable than he had felt in a while. A foolish grin tugged at his lips in response. "I'll see you soon."

As Beecroft hurried away, Victor couldn't help but notice that the earl was nicely proportioned and clearly fit. He drew in a shuddering breath, stunned that he'd gone from expecting an uneventful night to meeting for a tryst in less than a quarter hour. He barely knew Lord Beecroft and here he was about to indulge.

He stood and collected his folio from the chair, fumbling through the papers to make sure he'd not jumbled them too badly in his haste. He hadn't finished his calculations and for a brief moment he was tempted to complete them before he headed upstairs to join Beecroft. It wouldn't take long.

When he looked up, Lord Hambly stood next to him, a disapproving scowl on his face. "I see you're still *working*," he said, scorn tingeing his words with a hard edge.

Victor ignored the complaint. During their time together, Hambly had griped about his work so often that he was no longer made uncomfortable. A lord with very few responsibilities of his own, Hambly hadn't been able to accept Victor's work was important to him and had become more of a nuisance than a desired companion. He'd become so difficult that Victor had needed to end the relationship. "It's nice to see you too."

The viscount glanced him over; heat and desire clear in his expression. "I miss you, kitten."

Victor grimaced at the nickname. He'd hated the way Hambly had frequently made him feel low because of his preference to be the passive partner in bed. He made decisions every day in his work and when he was with a man he didn't want to discuss to the point of angry argument about what they would or would not do together. "It's over. Why can you not accept that?"

Hambly crowded him. "Because you belong with me."

Victor shook his head at Hambly' refusal to see the truth and shoved past him. Sexual relations between them had always been fraught with tension and Victor felt no regret over ending things last year. He didn't want to fight with a lover because he wouldn't fuck them. He was sick and tired of men who couldn't be affectionate during intimacy too.

He hardly knew Beecroft, but something in the way he smiled gave him hope that he might be the sort of man he needed in his life. At least for tonight.

CHAPTER TWO

Daniel Wellham, eighth Earl of Beecroft, rubbed his hands together, rather pleased with his evening plans. The room was perfect: warm without being too hot, a large bed to play upon, and a writing desk to the side where Victor Knight could work if he needed to. Daniel was aware he'd interrupted the man's habits tonight, but after a few minutes of indecision, he'd braved a rebuff and approached Mr. Knight's table directly. In the past, his efforts to strike up a conversation had failed where the delicious Mr. Knight had been concerned. He'd tried a new more forthright approach tonight despite the very likely possibility he'd be sent from London soon by his superiors.

Mr. Knight had responded well to his interruption and his rather coarse invitation to have sex tonight had been taken up with gratifying enthusiasm. Now, he'd get to find out more of the reserved man's nature. He truly knew little of Mr. Knight's peccadillos other than he was interested in men but had no current lover. Knight's liaisons had been few and discreet over the past years.

He worked too much. He ate too little.

Neither of those two points detracted from his appeal.

Victor was handsome, neat and had the softest of blue eyes hiding behind his wire-rimmed spectacles. Daniel got hard just thinking of revealing them when they went to bed together.

With nothing left to do, he fidgeted. What was keeping Mr. Knight? Had he returned to finish with his facts and figures before coming up?

Not that Daniel would mind. He hadn't lied that he admired Mr. Knight's dedication. He just hoped the banker hadn't had a change of heart about joining him and left him waiting.

He glanced around in relief as the door swung open quietly. Mr. Knight crossed the threshold; his folder clutched tightly to his side as always, a slight frown creasing his brow. That expression of irritation hadn't been present before. Was he now annoyed about the interruption?

Daniel crossed the room, closed and locked the door. "Would you prefer to finish your work first? I don't mind waiting."

Victor Knight's lips parted as he gaped. "Wait?"

Daniel moved close to him and grinned. "I take it you've not heard that often."

"Never." The man took a moment to consider his offer then shook his head. "Work can be delayed a few hours."

"Well, perhaps later tonight you could make use of that table over there to finish what I interrupted if the mood strikes," Daniel offered in all seriousness.

Mr. Knight regarded him a few moments, his brow creasing again, and then moved to set his folio atop the desk. Had Daniel's offer been that uncommon? Honestly, he had no qualms over waiting for the banker because he had a feeling the man would be worth any inconvenience of a delay.

Knight shrugged out of his coat to hang over the back of a chair. His movements revealed a narrow pair of hips and pert bottom encased in well-fitted trousers. Daniel's cock twitched. He might be willing to wait, but his cock didn't really want to. He'd been aroused from the moment he'd sat opposite the man in the dining room.

He moved to stand behind him and slid one palm over Knight's shoulder to prevent him from removing any more clothes. Daniel wanted that job. He wanted the pleasure of getting close to the banker's very skin. "Allow me."

A soft shudder shook the other man and he didn't resist when Daniel drew him against his chest. The plain and sensible waistcoat opened to his skillful fingers. The tight knot at his throat proved a little less compliant, but that too fell away.

They were close in height; Daniel being a touch

taller, and he traced the tips of his fingers over the base of Victor's throat above his shirt as he breathed deep. Anticipation raced through his limbs, but he didn't want to hurry getting to know what Mr. Knight liked when it came to intimacy. He wanted to take his time and bring them both the greatest pleasure possible. "What scent of cologne do you wear, Mr. Knight?"

"I... I don't," Mr. Knight stuttered. "It's simply the scent of soap you detect. A client's housekeeper sends it to me from time to time. I've no idea what it is."

Daniel slid his fingers up the other man's throat and he urged him to turn. "It suits you."

Mr. Knight's eyebrows rose in surprise. "Thank you."

Daniel removed Knight's wire-rim spectacles next, set them atop his folio and found those soft blue eyes even more arousing up close. "You have such pretty eyes." He grinned as bright color stole up Victor's cheeks. He saw little point in hiding the facets of Victor's appearance that attracted him most. He was as honest as he could be when it came to his lovers. About anything else in his life he must be vague.

After all, a spy didn't live very long if he didn't keep some secrets.

The flush of color to Victor's cheeks grew and he said nothing for a long time. Eventually, he murmured thanks and dropped his gaze. His pale lashes fanned across his skin, delicate and lovely.

Daniel squeezed Victor's arm, finding the limbs firm despite the hours the banker must spend bent over his papers. "You're not used to compliments, are you?"

"Flattery isn't necessary in these matters."

Daniel leaned closer, staring at Knight's lips. "But I do mean every word."

It didn't matter who moved first, but it was clear in that first kiss the banker liked another man taking control. He curled into Daniel eagerly, allowing him to lead, to embrace him and hold him against his chest. Knight's kiss was sweet, persistent and Daniel was moved enough by his surrender to tenderly cup his face.

He grew aware of his trousers being unbuttoned, his

shirt being tugged free and then Knight caressed his sides and lower back. He had soft hands, hands of a man who worked with pen and ink rather than the roughness of leather reins, or the abrasion of manual labors as Daniel was often forced to do in his line of work. Victor skimmed lightly up and down his spine and Daniel groaned as goose flesh raced over his skin. He preferred a gentle lover in his bed and Mr. Knight was certainly that. As arousing as hell though. His cock was so hard he was glad his trousers were unbuttoned or he'd be in pain.

Daniel backed Mr. Knight to the bed and gently pushed him down. Those blue eyes followed his every movement, awash with silent encouragement and anticipation. Daniel toed off his boots then stripped off his trousers. He would leave his shirt in place until the candle was blown to delay discussing the consequences of his secret life in too much detail for the present moment.

Knight lifted one leg to remove his own footwear, but Daniel performed the task for him as efficiently as any valet. The man had nicely formed calves and long feet. He couldn't wait to see the rest.

As he moved to join Mr. Knight on the bed, the man sat up, stripping off his shirt so he was naked from the waist up. When he lay back down with a sigh of contentment, Daniel decided to brave the questions sooner rather than later and removed his shirt too before joining him.

The banker wriggled until they were both comfortably entwined, a hand resting on Daniel's chest. He jerked his head back to stare a moment later. He grazed the edge of an old wound.

Knight's gaze flickered over the scars on his chest, his eyes widening. "You've been hurt."

Should have blown the candle out first. Daniel caught Knight's chin and lifted it to draw his attention away from his old scars. Wounds that proclaimed his life a tad more dangerous than Daniel ever wanted anyone to realize. "Try to forget them if you can."

The banker resisted. He came closer, skimming his fingers over each old wound very carefully.

Daniel groaned, both from pleasure of being touched and irritation. He couldn't explain the circumstances of receiving any of them, least of all the most noticeable. There was a slash across his chest, left collarbone to right nipple from a knife fight in Le Havre, an ugly round scar from a pistol shot that had healed badly, and the brand of a fire poker across his right forearm from a brief struggle with an assassin in Plymouth.

Eventually, Knight met his gaze. "I can't forget them. They are part of who you are."

"They were a duty." Daniel shook his head at his slip of the tongue and kissed the man in his arms, determined to have this interlude of pleasure with no further thought to the difficulties of his past or the uncertainty of his future. Thankfully, Knight's curiosity was easily turned aside by kisses and the man speared his fingers into Daniel's hair, encouraging his passions to increase.

They were a good fit together in bed, neither too large nor long against the other, both enjoying the soft tenderness of caressing each other as a precursor to deeper intimacy.

At exactly the moment it seemed right, Knight loosened his own trousers, nudged them down his hips. Daniel took hold of his cock in a firm, warm grip. The banker mimicked him and their sure strokes aroused each other enough they moaned in unison.

He allowed it for a little while then rose to his knees, caught hold of Knight's trousers and ripped them down his thighs a little more enthusiastically than he'd intended to.

Far from appearing offended at his haste, Knight chuckled softly, brought his feet together so the garment could be removed fully without damage. Once they were gone, he lay on his back, widened his legs and invited Daniel into his arms.

Instead, Daniel took a moment to admire the banker. Smooth sculpted skin, flawless white without any evidence he toiled over a desk. A light dusting of hair around his nipples and a tantalizing line leading to his groin. His cock was similar in size to Daniel's and his mouth watered in anticipation of having him deep in his throat. He skimmed his fingers over Knight's inner thigh and the man's cock twitched. "You are so pale." And damn sexy lying so abandoned on the equally white sheets.

His breath hissed out as Knight caught his cock, played with him. Strokes that made him flex his hips to mimic slowly fucking him.

"And you are so tanned. How does a lord of the realm spend so much time with his bare skin exposed to the sun?"

Daniel bit his lip. His relationships usually went downhill in proportion to how many questions he refused to answer. His duty to the Crown was a curse to his love life. He'd like to open his heart and confess every facet of his days, but he would never be free to do so. Secrecy and discretion were second nature now and he had become adept at brushing aside questions. "I'd like to see you bare chested in the sun one day."

Knight's smile dimmed. "I'll never find the time."

"How is the bank these days?"

This time it was Knight who bit his lip and seemed uncomfortable. His lids lowered, hiding his eyes. His cock lost some of its stiffness too. "I prefer not to discuss business matters if you don't mind," he said quietly.

Daniel nodded although aware Knight couldn't see. Perhaps they had another thing in common. The inner workings of a banking establishment should be kept confidential. He had no serious interest in the bank accept that was where Knight spent much of his time. But since neither of them was free to talk about the life they had apart from each other perhaps there was no need for friction. At least not at first. "A wise precaution. Let us agree not to discuss that which must not be given voice."

The banker glanced up swiftly, his smile one of relief. "Thank you." Knight stretched up, caught Daniel about the neck and pulled him down for another kiss.

As the kiss grew deeper, more erotic, he ached to fill Knight. His lover had a talented tongue and he worked it between Daniels lips in a perfect and graphic imitation of fucking. He was unsurprised by his growing hunger for this serious man. If they kept kissing like this, he'd spill his seed long before he ever claimed him.

He glanced to the side of the bed and spied a small vial of oil that was a feature of every pleasure room in the club.

Knight rolled onto his stomach, stretched for the bottle and passed it over his shoulder to Daniel. When he remained on his stomach, pale rounded arse presented, Daniel smiled in delight and caressed the base of Knight's spine. The man moaned when he scratched lightly with his nails and widened his legs a bit more.

They *were* a good match in bed. The matter of who would fuck whom didn't even need to be discussed. Knight was willing to receive. His trust was humbling and that just made Daniel's cock harder.

Daniel grabbed a pillow and stuffed it beneath Knight's hips, flicking his fingers along the length of Knight's shaft only briefly. He intended to bring them off together once he was inside the other man.

He sat back on his heels and filled his palm with oil. He liberally coated his cock with the thick liquid. Anticipation made the experience far too exciting, so he took his hand away. He'd long wondered about the quiet banker and he wasn't about to let anything else get between them.

He drizzled some at the top of Knight's arse, chuckling as the man squirmed as the oil slid downward. Daniel opened the cheeks of Knight's arse wider with his thumbs and leaned down to blow across the tight pucker. Knight jerked beneath him; a soft growl filled the room. "Shh," Daniel soothed as he drizzled even more oil there and slipped the tip of his finger inside. The banker pushed back, sinking Daniel's finger deep immediately.

He worked his digit in and out, delighted that the man pushed back into every touch, a ragged moan rumbling from his mouth. Before Daniel was ready to stop, Knight rose to his knees. He sank two fingers in next, noting the ease, and then inserted one more.

He stared at the arse waiting before him. The man

was as open as anyone he'd ever had. Daniel removed his fingers and set the head of his cock against that slicked hole. He pressed in slowly, anticipating some resistance but found little. He took a deep breath to steady his rioting senses as he sank balls deep easily on the first thrust. For a man who'd had only a handful of lovers in the last year Knight was remarkably giving to this kind of invasion.

Daniel drew back and then thrust again, repeating the movement until he was absolutely sure of Knight's contentment. He wanted to take his time and make certain Knight would want to see him again.

"Stop teasing and fuck me," Knight growled suddenly, turning to look over his shoulder. His blue eyes blazed bright with such fierce desire that Daniel was rendered speechless. He had assumed too much of Knight's quiet strength would linger in their bed play. He had forgotten the man was also direct. Clearly, Knight didn't hesitate in anything once he set his mind to it and for that he was grateful.

Released from the need to go slow, Daniel poured his lust, energy and passions into his movements. Knight appeared well used to being taken, something Daniel had less experience with, and demanded everything Daniel could give. The bed ropes groaned, the very frame creaked and the room was filled with the sweet sound of flesh slapping against flesh. Daniel ignored it as best he could in the hope of prolonging the act.

Sweat soon glistened over them both and Daniel rubbed his hands over Knight's slick, pale back, gripping his hips tightly a moment before touching him again.

He reached around Knight's hips, caught his cock at the base, and worked his flesh fast, keeping time with his own thrusts. The harder Daniel's thrusts grew the more Knight seemed to like it. He moaned and grunted with each slap of flesh against flesh.

He pulled at Knight's shoulders until he rose to his knees, then wrapped an arm about his chest to fit them together tightly. Knight jerked and cried out. Spilled seed warmed Daniel's fist and he came too with a suddenness that left him reeling.

They swayed on their knees, Daniel holding Knight tightly against his chest so he could kiss the banker's neck. Knight held Daniel's arm around him. Eventually, he sighed and settled to the bed in an untidy sprawl. Daniel followed, lying heavily over his lover while he caught his breath. For a last minute decision to act on his attraction to the quiet banker, their tryst couldn't have been more perfect if he'd planned it.

CHAPTER THREE

Victor rubbed the back of his neck. How the devil had they lost two more clients in the last seven days? There had been no need for Lord Forsythe to feel unhappy with the return on his investments. The account had actually been ahead of David Hawke's initial predictions.

"Can you see an error?" David Hawke asked, breaking the silence of his office at their modest premises on Lombard Street in London.

He smiled reassuringly to his business partner of ten years. "There's nothing wrong that I can see."

Hawke had inherited his share of the business from his father, as Victor had done from his own, and they were both aware they had much to live up to. They devoted long hours to the business and the idea either one of them might have made an error set them both on edge.

Hawke settled into his chair with a heavy sigh. "Thank God for that. We have auditors coming tomorrow to look over the other accounts. I'm at a loss to understand where we were supposed to have made this so-called mistake."

Anger filled Victor. If there was nothing wrong with the calculations then he was at a loss to know why Forsythe would think them in error. It may be merely paranoia on his part, but he was starting to feel uncomfortable. Was some unknown party spreading lies about their business dealings to drive clients away? The few that had withdrawn their investments and offered an explanation had strongly hinted, but never come right out and accused, their investments were in danger of misuse.

So far, the desertion was confined to a handful of accounts, but that trickle could soon become a spillway if they did not have every penny and pound accounted for by a reputable and impartial audit to offer proof of their professionalism. Hawke was taking the accusations just as badly and he smiled at the man to reassure him they were in this together. "I am confident all is in order and the audit tomorrow will uncover nothing untoward."

"Then why is this happening?"

"I don't know. Listen Hawke, I know you won't want to hear it, but there's nothing left to do tonight. Take yourself home to your wife, enjoy your evening together, and I will see you tomorrow. Give my regards to Abigail and thank her for her kindness in sending luncheon today. I will straighten all of this up before I head home."

Although unhappy at the idea of leaving, Hawke couldn't resist the lure of returning home to his wife. Mrs. Abigail Hawke was exactly what his partner had needed. She brightened Hawke's life and made him smile much more often than Victor had ever observed before. Victor had grown very fond of her too. She was very easy to talk to, though she had no interest in finance.

Victor neatened the papers on his desk, gathered the files and locked them away until tomorrow. He was weary and dreaded the trek to the club to beg for dinner at this late hour. But since there was nothing at home worth considering as edible, he had no choice. Besides, there was always the chance he might run into Lord Beecroft again tonight. A word or two of explanation about his absence might be in order, if the earl had noticed he'd not been around the club for days.

"You really do work until all hours."

Victor spun to find the man in question propped against his doorway. The earl smiled and slowly swung an overburdened basket to and fro at his side. "I thought you might be hungry."

He stared at the man in relief. "Beecroft, you might have just saved me from having Marinari ring a peel over my head for being late to dinner. Thank you."

Lord Beecroft was a sight for sore eyes and he considered kissing him in greeting, but he wasn't sure how that sort of thing would go over. They'd only met for sex once. What had the earl made of his lack of attendance at the club these past days? Given he was here now, with an offering of food, he didn't appear too upset with him. "I was thinking about you today."

Beecroft's smile grew as his gaze dipped lower. "Just today?"

"Well." Victor's cock thickened in response to the earl's scrutiny. He couldn't help it. Beecroft had been a generous lover and had occupied much of his thoughts in his spare moments. He glanced at the door, realizing the space beyond was dark and silent. "I didn't hear you speak to my partner on his way out."

Beecroft set the basket on the table and started removing items. "I didn't want to trouble him with explaining who I was since I'm not a client. I waited until he was long gone before coming in."

Victor hurried for his office door. "Wasn't the entrance locked?"

"Of course." Lord Beecroft cleared his throat. "I've, ah, not come across a lock that can keep me out as yet."

Victor stared at the earl in shock. He'd picked the lock? Dear God, what sort of man had he gotten involved with? Curiosity about Lord Beecroft's life, the scars, his lock picking ability and his frequent disappearances from Society burned his tongue. They had agreed to avoid uncomfortable topics of conversation between them and this likely was one that touched on parts of Lord Beecroft's life that Victor wasn't sure he wanted to know.

Lord Beecroft watched him silently then shrugged. "Would you be more comfortable if I offered to leave?"

"You could simply come back later." Victor regretted his words as soon as he spoke them. He'd just accused an earl of ungentlemanly behavior and that sort of thing was never taken lightly.

Rather than be offended, Beecroft chuckled softly. "But I would not come back if you were not here, Mr. Knight. I came to see the man, not the money in his vaults."

Reassured by his comment somewhat, Victor relaxed

a bit. Just because a man *could* pick a lock didn't mean he *would* use that skill for his own gain. He could at least give Lord Beecroft the benefit of the doubt for now. So far, the man had been direct and truthful. He moved to Beecroft's side and examined the food being laid out on his desk. His stomach rumbled. "This is very kind."

"I didn't know what you'd like, but there is duck, oysters, bread and something sweet too." He opened a bottle of wine and produced a single glass. He poured and handed it over. "For you."

Victor shared the wine and glass with Lord Beecroft, eating with his fingers and conscious his lover was silent. He wiped his mouth. "I'm sorry I haven't had time to come to the club."

Lord Beecroft eyes widened. "I've been away too."

Victor burst out laughing then quickly stifled the sound.

"Do you think it's funny?" Lord Beecroft crowded him against the desk. "I was worried you'd think I didn't care to see you again."

"I must confess I worried for similar reasons."

Lord Beecroft's eyes softened and he leaned in for a kiss. A delicious thrill swept through Victor. He hadn't met a lover outside of the club in a long time and never one in his place of business. There were dangers associated with public displays of affection between men. But in the privacy of his office, after regular business hours, it was too tantalizing a situation to halt.

He held his lover against him, delighting when Lord Beecroft cupped his face as they kissed. Daniel had done that quite often the other night. He seemed a tactile, gentle man when it came to passion. Victor burrowed into his warmth and strength, hoping the earl might want more from him. His cock throbbed impatiently to be touched.

Eventually, they drew apart, although Victor didn't want to. Lord Beecroft delivered a tidbit of duck to his mouth and fed him. Victor blushed. He'd never had a man feed him before either. "I can do it myself."

"I want to do it. Your lips fascinate me. Such

economy of expression, yet your kiss speaks volumes to me." Beecroft brushed a slither of cheese across his bottom lip. "Open for me."

He did as asked, self-consciously chewing and swallowing what he'd been given. Next came another sip of wine, then bread, duck and more cheese. Victor glanced at the oysters, curious why he'd been denied them so far.

Lord Beecroft noted the direction of his gaze. "I wasn't sure what my reception would be given it's been several nights since we've seen each other. They say oysters do wonders for a man's libido."

"Given my cock is hard as a rock now, I don't think I need any help in that area," Victor told him honestly.

"Neither will I, but it's too late to throw them back." Lord Beecroft smirked, and then dipped his head to nuzzle Victor's jaw. "Shall we indulge here or will you invite me to spend the night with you? We could go to the club."

"Here might be expedient, but there is too great a risk my partner might return after dining with his wife," Victor murmured. He would not like to be caught in a compromising position and ruin a perfectly satisfactory business partnership with the truth of his sexual preferences. "Come home with me instead. My building is closer than the club."

The earl smiled broadly. "I'd love to."

Beecroft served him several oysters, took two for himself, and then started to pack everything away again. Victor snatched up a few more morsels then completed straightening up his office. When he was done, Lord Beecroft was waiting patiently at the office door.

"My lord, if you will come this way."

His lover pressed a kiss to his cheek and then moved to the entrance so Victor could lock up the office properly. They set off on the short walk to his home at a leisurely pace. As Victor strolled along, he had the urge to curl his arm through Beecroft's as some of the braver fellows did while walking around the privacy of the club together, declaring their amours to one and all. Behavior like that in public would cause problems if they were recognized so he curled his hands into fists at his sides instead. Discretion was the wiser choice and safer.

Lord Beecroft was silent until they reached his home. Victor owned the building, a recent purchase, but his apartment consisted of the floor and attic above the milliner's shop he'd leased out. It wasn't particularly grand or in the best address, but his home was comfortable and had a private side entrance that allowed any visitors discretion as they came and went. Not that he'd had visitors yet. He'd been much too busy of late for socializing.

He unlocked and allowed Lord Beecroft to precede him, eager to continue what they'd started before. "We are alone."

Once a candle had been lit, Beecroft glanced around his sitting room; his eyes narrowed on the stack of crates Victor hadn't had time to unpack since moving in. With a shock of discomfort, Victor realized he'd been meaning to deal with them for ages. The room had a just moved in feel despite him living here for seven months. "I'll get around to finishing unpacking. Do excuse the mess, my lord."

"Daniel," Beecroft said at last, with a slight shake of his head.

"I beg your pardon?"

"Call me by my name. Daniel."

Lord Beecroft's request brought a smile to his lips. "I am Victor."

"I know. Well, now we have our introductions out of the way I suggest you strip down to your bare skin, bend over the end of your bed, and—" Daniel caressed Victor's bottom—"part those glorious cheeks of yours. You can blame the oysters for my impatience."

"Gladly and I'll do the same."

Daniel followed him through the cluttered living space to the bedchamber at the back of the apartment. Victor stripped himself as quickly as he could, discarding his clothes carelessly as anticipation filled him. When he was naked, he placed his hands flat on the mattress, pushing his bottom out the way Daniel had requested.

His lover caressed his arse and the sensation of nails gently teasing the base of his spine curled his toes. "Oil?"

Victor sucked in a sharp breath and widened his feet on the floor. "Top drawer of the dresser behind you."

The drawer rattled open and Daniel chuckled. "Quite the collector."

He glanced behind him and grinned. Daniel was naked now too, his cock full and red, seed sliding down the shaft. The earl juggled three dildos of varying sizes from the drawer, his expression fascinated. "You may try as many as you care for."

"Which do you prefer?"

"You." He faced the bed. "Your cock suits me better than those implements. I only use them when I am without a lover."

That had been often lately.

"Maybe later," Daniel murmured as he again caressed Victor's bottom.

His balls tightened. The way Daniel touched him in all the right places made him impatient. "I just want you."

"I meant for you to fill me with one later tonight if the mood struck," Daniel clarified.

Victor glanced over his shoulder and grinned. "Whatever you want."

Daniel had hold of his cock, slowly stroking the length while watching him. Victor's legs trembled at the heat in his expression. The last time, they'd not glimpsed each other's expressions often and when faced with Daniel's obvious lust Victor was in danger of coming from that look alone.

The earl parted his cheeks and stabbed into him without preamble. Victor rose up on his toes, but the earl's hand landing softly on his spine calmed him. His thrusts were urgent, yet not rough, forcing Victor to brace himself against the bed. A hard fuck after a troubling day was exactly what he needed. Daniel was so slick and hard that soon the slap of bare, sweaty skin filled the chamber. Victor lifted one knee to rest upon the bed. The change of position brought a growl of hunger from his lover and his thrusts grew frantic.

Victor grasped his cock as his lover shouted out his release, denying him a chance to come with him this time round.

He lowered his foot to the floor again, squeezed the cock where it rested inside him, while he stroked his own flesh.

Daniel's breath was rough as he kissed Victor's shoulder. "I'm laying the blame for coming so soon on the oysters."

Victor tipped his head back as his release drew close. He didn't mind Daniel coming first as he was still firm inside him. "And here I thought I was simply too exciting for you," he teased.

"You are exciting to be around," Daniel promised. "I'm mad for you and I'll prove it."

The earl pulled out so suddenly that Victor protested the loss of sensation. He needed more to come. Daniel spun him around, pressed him to sit on the edge of the bed, and knocked his hand away from his aching length. Then Daniel dropped to his knees between his parted thighs and took the tip of his cock into his mouth. Having a peer, an earl, service him was a first. Usually they were fussy about sucking cock and Daniel's eagerness pleased him. His lover met his gaze and Victor panted at the mischievous expression he wore. The man was so bloody confident. So forthright in his passions and that aroused Victor unbearably.

He groaned as the earl took the whole length of his cock deep enough into his throat so he could massage the head as he swallowed. Victor was familiar with the technique, having pleasured others this way before, but he'd never been on the receiving end. The unfamiliar sensations were too much, too exciting, and Victor lasted barely a half-minute before he lost control. He came and loudly, an unusual reaction for him. He clutched Daniel's shoulder for balance as his cock was milked dry and then licked from root to tip with more care and attention than he'd ever been shown before.

When Daniel released him, Victor flopped backward on the bed and lay there sated and content. "Please do that again one day when I haven't eaten oysters. I want to have a modicum of control in my possession next time."

"Most assuredly there will be a next time. You're perfect for me." Daniel climbed onto the bed as well, curling onto his side close by. Victor reached to touch him, and was pleased when Daniel tangled his fingers in his hair with a gentle caress. "I like being with you, Vic. Very much so."

Victor grinned, pleased to know he wasn't alone in his satisfaction. He was glad to have taken a chance on the earl. "Is that so?"

"Hmm," Daniel murmured. "I like how eager you are for me and that you don't ask too many questions."

He glanced at the scars on Daniel's chest briefly then met his gaze. "Don't mistake my lack of questions for indifference. I do want to know more about you."

The earl nodded, and his face grew serious. "I will tell you what you need to know."

So there would be more secrets between them if they were to continue together. Picking locks, sudden absences, old scars. Unanswered questions. Victor struggled with an explanation and he couldn't dismiss it immediately. Daniel lived a dangerous life. But why? He was an earl, a popular man in Society. He was respected. Victor couldn't imagine him a bad man. He'd never be working *against* England, which meant he might be working *for* his country. A spy? "I think I might understand."

Daniel's eyes glowed as he smiled warmly, then he pulled Victor against him. He inhaled deeply. "I'm going to steal a bar of your soap so that when we are apart I have a remembrance."

Victor rested his cheek on his chest, disturbed by the idea Daniel believed they'd part ways. "Will that be soon?"

There was a long pause and then Daniel sighed. "Yes and often." He kissed his brow once, and then repeated the gesture.

Victor was filled with uncertainty, but one thought was clear—whatever Daniel did when he was away from Society was dangerous, and ongoing. The idea of his lover's life in peril brought acute anxiety, despite their short association. Victor hadn't planned to care for the earl but in the short time they'd spent together it seemed his heart had foolishly gotten ahead of reason. Every moment together could be their last and there was only one thing to do. "Well, then, we had better make the most of tonight. We'll need more oysters."

CHAPTER FOUR

The branch of the government Daniel worked for was so secret that it operated out of an upstairs apartment above a gentleman's tailoring business in the center of the great city of London to avoid scrutiny of their actions from those of gentler sensibilities. Many a death and interrogation had been arranged here, all that was missing was blood staining on the hardwood floors as evidence. Daniel didn't imagine many were innocent of their crimes. By intent or blunder, those who shared England's secrets were usually found out and dealt with swiftly.

The industrious workshops below did actually make fine clothing, some of which Daniel wore in his everyday life as an earl. But the tailor also designed the disguises he was required to wear when engaged in business for the Crown, right down to the authenticity of food stains and the odd fleck of tar jammed beneath his nails.

Daniel hadn't enjoyed his time as a deckhand aboard an enemy ship last month very much at all, but sacrifices had to be made. He'd been making them all his adult life and he was surprised every day by seeing another end.

He forced relaxation over his body as he sat before his two immediate superiors in a room so spare of features and curios that even he, if he ever returned without forewarning, would dismiss it as nothing but a disused room. He crossed his long legs at the ankle, doing his best to appear nonchalant about this meeting, but all his senses were tingling a warning for caution. Lord Pickens, a new face promoted into their ranks recently, had summoned him and appeared unusually gruff. "Where is he?"

Pickens would only ask Daniel about one man.

Beside Lord Pickens, Lord Freeport, the man who had recruited him long ago looked on without revealing alarm at the question posed and that worried Daniel all the more. Freeport knew the answer to The Angel's whereabouts as well as Daniel did.

He fought the urge to react with any sudden movement that might hint at discomfort. "The Angel hasn't been in London for many months. He moves a great deal, as you knew he would." He hoped his subterfuge was still easily believed. The Angel was in London. He hadn't changed residence in years.

"Well, he's not in bloody Wales where he was reported to be last month," Lord Pickens growled, his face turning red in anger. "Half the world is looking for him and you were the last to see him."

The Angel, an assassin of considerable skill, had once been eager to be at His Majesty's beck and call. Some might claim he was a myth, a lure to attract bright young men into the life of a spy. The Angel was actually flesh and blood. A cheeky morsel who drove everyone he met to distraction, but in recent months had grown resistant to his real line of work.

Depending on your point of view The Angel was either an assassin or a procurer of wicked delight at the Hunt Club's upper rooms. Angelo Marinari's kills were quickly done. His flirtations were said to leave a man reeling. A more complicated fellow one could never find. Daniel had given up trying to discover what was fact and what was fantasy long ago. "That was months ago now. He's moved again I'm sure and I have every confidence he will contact me as arranged."

Daniel didn't wish to lie, but he'd promised Marinari he'd do all he could to extract him from this devil's bargain. The man was bone tired of the killing, haunted by regrets and in danger of losing his mind, in Daniel's opinion. There was cause to hope Marinari yet. He was not a bad man, though his moral compass could be described as severely bent.

He had fallen in love and fallen hard. That gave Daniel hope.

"I want him found and brought to me." Lord Pickens smacked his fist into his palm, his eyes wild as he stared across the battered cutting table. "The Crown has placed a price on his head. One thousand pounds if he's brought in alive."

Daniel struggled to hide his confusion at the news and keep his gaze away from Lord Freeport. Since that man knew where Marinari had been all along he could have easily supplied the answer and spared the expense and effort of a manhunt. Daniel chose his words with care. "The Angel swore allegiance to His Majesty absolutely. Pledged never to kill or hurt on English soil unless it's by royal decree and you're turning against him because he doesn't come to heel the moment you've snapped your fingers. He is one of us."

Lord Pickens's gaze grew flat with suspicion. "It's been four months since he's been *one of us*. For all we know The Angel is gathering intelligence about England and selling it to the highest bidder. We lost ten good men in Cornwell."

Daniel didn't bother to hide his anger at the reminder of that near disastrous mission last month. He'd been there, but too late. "Some of those men I counted as friends. If I thought The Angel could be involved do you not think I would have dealt with him in the same fashion?"

"No one is doubting your integrity," Lord Freeport murmured quickly, breaking his silence for the first time. "That said, it is time for The Angel to follow every order, as we all must do."

Marinari would never agree, but for Daniel to reveal his greater understanding of the man would lead others to question just how often they did meet. "I will contact him through usual channels."

"See that you do and then bring him here to me," Pickens demanded in a voice so edged with frustration and anger that a chill swept the room.

Daniel froze. "Here?"

"Yes, here." Lord Pickens's stabbed a finger into the rough tabletop, his gaze determined and setting off a clamor of warning bells in Daniel's mind. Marinari had always operated outside official and even unofficial channels. He walked a fine line to be sure, but bringing him here would undoubtedly risk certain exposure. He glanced at Freeport to see just how lost his cause was. The man nodded and Daniel's heart sank.

The Angel would rather die than be captured again.

There were more governments than the British who wanted Marinari in their power. Daniel would never bring him here. That was one order he'd disobey.

Instead of saying what he thought, he nodded. "As you wish."

Distaste filled him as he took his leave. Alliances had been subtly shifting inside the group and if Freeport agreed with Pickens then Daniel didn't know whom to trust now. He trudged downstairs with a heavy heart, his mind filled with worry. He didn't like not knowing what was happening. That was why he'd survived so long as a spy.

He slipped into the tailor's storefront and browsed the glass-fronted cabinets, as was his habit after meeting to discuss his missions. The proprietor Mr. Brody smiled in welcome and slipped up the back stairs, leaving an assistant behind a counter to attend Daniel. Thankfully, the assistant remained silent while he perused the latest in buttons and collected his thoughts. He had to warn Marinari that his life was again in danger and decide what to do next. He moved on, without liking any of the buttons or his options for Marinari.

At the shop counter, he spied embroidered handkerchiefs and idly flipped through them, admiring the craftsmanship with half his mind. But his attention caught on one monogramed with a V. The lettering was done in blue, to match Victor's eyes, so he impulsively paid for it and with just one purchase, went on his way.

Outside, Bond Street was awash with activity and he meandered through the crowd with little thought to his final destination. He perused the bookshop but saw nothing that captured his interest. He bought a pastry in a little bakery and munched on that. Before long he spied Hawke and Knight Bank up ahead.

Was it wise, or even acceptable, to call on a lover during the day at his place of business?

He'd never done so before, but he was filled with restlessness where his lover was concerned. Victor had booted him out before the sun rose, claiming he had an exceptionally busy day ahead. Although they agreed not to question each other, Daniel was incredibly attuned to any evasiveness in others and his curiosity about what made today so important got the better of him.

He pushed open the bank door and stopped a few paces in. On first glance, the dark wood interior provided a reassuring comfort that here was a thriving, sound place of business. However, that first impression was soon demolished when one noted the tension crackling in the air. Around him clerks hurried to and fro in a barely restrained urgency. Daniel frowned at them as he removed his hat. He wasn't a client of the bank, but since he'd visited the establishment the night before he knew at least at night the place had been orderly.

Victor's office and his partners' were located at the rear. At the moment Victor's door was closed tight, but when he listened carefully could hear the murmur of voices rising in animated discussion inside.

He took another pace deeper into the premises and a clerk finally noticed him standing there. "May I help you, sir?"

Adopting the haughty mannerisms that always got him access to what he wanted, he waved toward the rear office door. "Lord Beecroft to see Mr. Knight if he has a moment to spare."

The other clerks froze and clutched their folders tightly to their chest.

The clerk who'd first addressed him drew himself up importantly. "Do you have an appointment?"

Daniel shook his head. "A spur of the moment decision to call."

The clerk edged closer, held one arm out in an attempt to steer him back toward a side desk. "He's terribly busy at the moment, my lord. Is there anything I can do for you in his place?"

"Hardly."

"Of course." The man almost genuflected in his

haste to be agreeable. "I am more than happy to make an appointment for you. It's not worth my life to disturb him today. Mr. Knight is in meetings with some very important people and I am not sure when he will be free to see you. Might I pass along a message or set up an appointment for you with him tomorrow?"

The door to Victor's office opened as a clerk slipped out and Daniel could see his lover's profile clearly beside his business partner, face pale, anxiety clear in every facet of his being. Something was terribly wrong. An overwhelming urge to ask those unspeakable questions about the bank's current status and future filled him.

The door swung shut, well before Victor could realize Daniel was standing outside. "No message or appointment. I will catch his notice another time if the impulse strikes me again."

The clerk appeared torn, both relieved he would go and likely disappointed at the loss of potential new business for the bank. "As you wish, my lord." The clerk gestured to the door, making it clear Daniel shouldn't linger where he had no business being.

However, Daniel was filled with an unfathomable urge to stay. To try to fix whatever was amiss. And why should he think he had that right? He'd only made love to Victor on two occasions. He wasn't the man's protector.

He slipped from the bank into the street, puzzled by how the serious man had begun to mean so much to him and so quickly. They barely knew each other and yet Victor dominated his thoughts.

Daniel stopped on the footpath outside Keppel & Sons Goldsmiths where a small collection of jewelry resided on royal blue velvet pillows in the windows. He was not usually so distracted by lovers. In his line of work it wasn't wise to form close connections with anybody, nor make long-term plans.

He stared at the items on display trying to understand his feelings. Victor wore no jewelry, not even a cravat pin at his neck. Daniel twisted the family signet ring on his finger as he considered what might be appropriate for the banker. He should own at least a signet ring. Daniel could have a pretty one made up one day and inscribed with their initials. He shook his head at the direction of his thoughts. What was he doing making plans for a future when he was never sure his work for the Crown could guarantee he had one?

As he glanced around, a reflection in the glass caught his attention. He noted the shape resolved itself into the form of the assistant from the tailors. The young man strode past with a bare nod of acknowledgement, entered a doorway a few shops away and vanished.

Years of service as a spy taught him not to ignore the sense of dread filling him. He left the goldsmiths, walked diagonally across the street, then checked the reflections in these new windows.

The assistant from the tailors shop followed him at a discreet distance. He gritted his teeth at the idea he was being watched. Lord Pickens, or was it Freeport, had set a spy on his trail, and although he was guilty of lying to them about The Angel's whereabouts, he found it unfair.

Daniel ducked into an alley, taking cover behind a stack of discarded crates. He kept silent and still, waiting and preparing for his next move. Annoyance turned to anger. His own country had set a spy upon him because he wouldn't deliver The Angel into their hands. Well, he was much too seasoned to allow that nonsense.

A thud of a hesitant tread was the only warning his stalker had followed him into the alley. *A new man in the game?* That could only be to his advantage. Not willing to cause too great an injury, Daniel reached for the tailor's assistant, caught his shoulders and slammed him into the nearest wall as hard as he could, stunning him.

The would-be spy collapsed in a heap when released, alive but insensible. Knowing he had to move and quickly, Daniel exited the alley and turned his steps toward the only refuge he could think of at short notice while he decided what he must do to ensure Marinari's continued safety.

CHAPTER FIVE

"Don't change one thing you're already doing," Mr. Fredrick Fallows advised as he shook Victor's hand firmly before taking his leave. When the door closed behind Mr. Fallows and his three-man audit team, both Victor and David Hawke collapsed into their chairs in Victor's office.

"Thank God that is over and done with," Hawke whispered.

Vindication was a heady feeling and he smiled broadly. Their affairs *were* in order. They even had letters of surety to now show to any of their existing clients who came to close their accounts in the future because they'd heard their investments were at risk. There was no cause for alarm. Far from it. Their business practices and profits had impressed the hell out of Fallows and his associates. Not one shilling was unaccounted for.

"I agree." Victor ran a hand through his hair, his elation dimming slightly. Nothing was explained as to why those former clients had come to the conclusion that the bank was going into a decline.

He glanced at his partner, noting the softening of his posture as he sprawled in his chair. The stress of their recent losses had taken its toll on each of them in different ways. According to Hawke's wife, his partner hadn't been sleeping particularly well. He looked exhausted now the assessment was over.

Victor poured them both a drink and sipped his, mulling over those past losses, racking his brain for any explanation. Had their competition decided to ruin them by spreading lies? If so, they were making a good attempt of it. And yet, of the clients who had taken their business elsewhere, they had nothing in common. Not background, not close connections, not even the institution they'd taken their money to after leaving

Hawke and Knight Bank. No one was particularly gaining in this nightmare. It made no sense.

With the source of their problems still unresolved, Victor couldn't rest on his laurels. He sipped his drink slowly, unable to feel at ease yet. He didn't want to disenchant Hawke tonight, but the matter was far from over. However, further discussion could wait until tomorrow. "You should go home."

Hawke stood. "Yes, an excellent idea. I'm going to flirt with my wife and I think I will have the best night's sleep since this whole mess started."

Victor grinned. Once upon a time, David Hawke had never spoken so candidly of his affections. Marrying Abigail had changed him in many subtle ways. He held up his hands. "Please spare me further details of your astounding good fortune. You *are* lucky to have her, so do not tarry here. Goodnight, my friend."

Hawke faced him. "You should get some rest too. You're looking a little frayed at the edges."

Who wouldn't with their reputations on the line? "No more than you."

"But being the older man, you're bearing the strain rather badly." Hawke shook his head. "I have Abigail to go home to. What do you have? A room full of boxes."

Hawke must be feeling lighter in spirit if he could tease. "You're married not two years and already attempting to give out advice for one's love life. Get away with you and I will see you in the morning, *young man*."

As Hawke slipped out the door, Victor lost his smile. He truly didn't have anyone but friends in his life, unless he counted the secretive Earl of Beecroft who came and went from Town with few explanations. Even so, Victor hoped to see him tonight. Perhaps they'd meet at the club and take a room again. The man was rather delicious and thoughtful when he was around.

Before he could collect his hat and depart for the club, one of the newer clerks approached, hat and coat at the ready to take his leave. "You had a visitor today, Mr. Knight. A Lord Beecroft called around two in the afternoon but would not leave a message. He had no appointment in the book and I don't recall that he's a client."

Daniel had called? Victor was both delighted and alarmed. He truly didn't want his troubles known to his lover so soon in their relationship, but he was pleased to have been sought out during the day at his place of business. "You are correct. He's not a client. Thank you for alerting me that he was here."

"Shall I make a tentative appointment for him and contact him by letter on your behalf?"

"No, I will deal with Lord Beecroft's inquiries personally." *Very personally.*

The clerk nodded and departed, leaving Victor alone in the bank as was normal for the evenings. When he thought of Daniel calling on him, a silly grin twisted his lips. Perhaps he did have someone to go home to after all. He wouldn't mind curling up against the earl in any bed.

When his day's final business was completed, Victor left his work folio behind for a change. He needed a breather, some perspective on his problem. A night of reflection might do him the world of good. He headed to the Hunt Club, hoping to see Lord Beecroft there and was pleased to discover he wasn't too late for the dinner hour.

The grand saloon held many familiar faces, but none of them were his current lover. He spoke to a few men but wasn't keen to linger. He wanted Daniel.

Disappointed not to find him quickly, Victor moved directly to the dining room since service had already commenced. Daniel wasn't there unfortunately.

He hoped his lover had not needed to disappear from Society again on some secret mission or whatnot, but it was a possibility. He supposed if he wanted any sort of relationship with that man he might have to accept there would be many more nights spent alone. He was used to being alone most of the time. He worked odd and long hours. As he surveyed the overflowing sideboard and made his choices for dinner, he kept an eye out for Daniel's appearance even while resigning himself to another night alone.

A footman heaped his plate, settled him at a table and procured a bottle of claret as he requested. Now he was sure all was in order financially, he would need all his strength to get to the bottom of any rumors. A hearty meal would help him think in new directions. As he began to eat in earnest, a hand settled over his shoulder and squeezed.

Victor glanced up, hoping for Daniel but discovering Viscount Hambly instead. His brilliant smile caused Victor's heart to sink. "Hambly." He wished the man would just go away. He didn't want to deal with a persistent former lover. His mind was on other matters. "What brings you to my table again?"

"I've missed you."

Victor froze, and then shook his head. It was over between them. "Will you be in London long?"

The viscount settled into the opposite chair. "As long as you need me."

He set his silver aside and wiped at his mouth to hide his frustration. Perhaps he'd not been forthright enough in the past about the reasons for their break. "I don't need you."

Hambly winced. "Yes, you do. More than ever. You need a friend who understands the troubles you're going through."

Victor frowned and waited for an explanation. He hadn't shared the problems at the bank with anyone.

The other man's gaze filled with pity. "You don't need to hide the truth from me. Everyone is talking about your little bank. It's that partner of yours, isn't it? I never liked him."

His former lover hadn't liked anyone in Victor's life. David Hawke's connections were too common for the viscount's tastes, and he'd barely been courteous when they'd met. But his heart still leaped to his throat at the mention of being talked about. It was the first time anyone had ever directly remarked on the solvency of Hawke and Knight Bank to him. Perhaps Hambly could help him solve the riddle of who was trying to destroy him. He kept his expression neutral. "What makes you think we are having problems?"

He shrugged. "Word gets around."

So there is a rumor? "There's nothing wrong at the bank."

"Yes, yes. By all means keep up appearances. I cannot help but notice you're missing your folio. I know you as well as I know myself. You don't go anywhere without those blasted bits of paper. You even took it to bed with us, if you recall." Hambly helped himself to Victor's claret. He took a sip then grimaced, setting the glass aside unfinished and scowled. "When did you begin drinking claret? Ghastly stuff."

Victor didn't bother to remind Hambly he'd always preferred claret with his dinner. Another facet of their relationship that hadn't worked and caused resentment on his part. Hambly had rarely remembered Victor had preferences that were not his own.

And it was true he'd taken his banking papers to bed with them, so he didn't bother to dispute that. He'd never been one to leave them far from his reach when outside the privacy of the bank, not even when Hambly had stayed over at his last home on rare occasions. Most often, he'd tucked the folio under the mattress on his side of the bed. "I'm taking a night off."

"The first of many, I suspect." Hambly leaned close. "Listen, a group of us was invited to a soiree at Freeport House. Since you're available tonight, why don't you come along as my guest? Freeport's a grand old fellow, quite charming all 'round but utterly clueless on the whole. It will be like old times and we can go home to your bed together afterward."

It might sound like fun were the circumstances and invitation from another person, but he wouldn't go anywhere as Hambly's guest and certainly not take him home to bed. He was involved with Lord Beecroft and until he was certain that affair had no future he would stay the course. "Thank you, but I have other plans for my evening."

"You mean with Beecroft." Hambly's nostrils flared as he took a breath. "Aiming a little high up the pecking order, aren't you? But I suppose he is a wealthy earl and well connected. Is your plan to cultivate some new clients from him and his set to replace the old?"

"Hardly." Distaste filled Victor at the suggestion he was interested in Daniel's money and connections. The earl had an entirely personal value to Victor. His lover may be wealthy, but Victor hadn't a clue about his true financial value. He didn't need to know. "When it comes to pleasure, wealth and title mean very little in the bedroom," Victor countered hotly. "That is all I want Lord Beecroft for."

A hiss of disagreement left Hambly. "You had no grounds for complaint with me. I had you more often than you had me."

Victor sat back in irritation and glanced around. He hadn't meant to start down this path in any discussion with his former lover but it always seemed to happen. Hambly hadn't grown out of his habit of keeping score, money, titles, degrees of attractiveness, especially in matters that related to the bedroom. It was ridiculous to have to justify his new relationship to Hambly, but he wouldn't stand to have his feelings for Daniel maligned.

He cared for Daniel. Of late, the memory of Daniel taking him so deep in his throat to bring him off made him swell with incautious desire wherever he happened to be. Daniel had made sex mean more than just a release too. He made love like it was fun, an adventure. A pleasant pastime shared. As he cast his gaze over Hambly, turned out to perfection should anyone of greater consequence look his way, he realized the man would never understand why Victor would always welcome Daniel over him. "My love life is none of your business."

"Love?" Hambly choked out, his face turning red.

Victor considered his reaction. Hambly didn't believe men should say they loved each other, but Victor had fallen in and out of love many times. He had with Hambly, in and out swiftly. But with Daniel and so soon? *Fancy that!* "Yes, love."

He grinned at the discovery. He had fallen in love with a man who was not afraid to say exactly what came to mind, especially sweet words of affection.

His affair with the Earl of Beecroft might have started out as a whim, but a deeper connection lurked beneath the pressure of his touch. Behind the merriment of his eyes was a definite hint they might have a future. Victor hoped for a long one.

"You don't know what he's really like," Hambly ground out through his clenched jaw. "He won't want you when your business is forced to close. How many clients have you lost now? Ten. A dozen."

The false rumors were spreading if Hambly had heard he'd lost a number of clients. His tally was not accurate but still too close for comfort. Hambly wasn't even a client of the bank, so it really was none of his business.

"You are right. I don't know Beecroft well. But I'm a patient enough man to find out his likes and dislikes, his opinions and character, for myself without listening to gossip." Victor considered what remained of his dinner but couldn't persuade himself to eat another morsel. "You should afford me the same courtesy."

"I am trying to help you," Hambly pleaded. "To spare you the burden alone."

"I'm not alone. I never have been." Victor stood, utterly unmoved by Hambly's offer of help. "Goodbye, Lord Hambly."

Hambly stood too. "You'll be back. When you fall, I'll be waiting to pick up the pieces. I will try not to remind you that I warned you not to bite off more than you could chew."

Victor didn't believe that for a moment. Hambly would rub any failure in his face. He would find perverse pleasure in his setbacks. God alone knew why he would want to do so. Perhaps he wished Victor to suffer because he had been the one to end their relationship. That had been the best decision Victor had ever made. "It was never me who bit hard enough to leave a mark. That was always your choice. Excuse me. I think I'd rather be alone than with you."

CHAPTER SIX

As the downstairs door to Victor's apartment opened, Daniel jumped to his feet, senses alert and tingling. He'd been waiting hours for Victor to come home and had been on the point of going in search of him. It was either that or unpack the boxes scattered 'round the room that were driving him insane with curiosity.

To pass the time, he'd read his way through weeks' worth of the *London Chronicle*. There had once been an untidy stack beside the cold hearth and he'd at last managed to catch up on Society news. He returned the last one on the tidy pile and stood.

His lover strode into the room, fingers pinching the bridge of his nose, knocking his glasses askew so badly he wouldn't be able to see the room around him clearly. His hair was unruly, his breath rough and rasping. Victor rubbed his face and heaved a heavy sigh as the door banged shut. "Alone again."

Clearly Victor didn't notice he wasn't.

Daniel coughed and Victor yelped out loud, spinning around, fists raised. "It's only me." He held his hands up in a gesture of peace and stepped forward. "It's Daniel."

Victor righted his glasses and glanced around, easily spotting him now he wasn't hidden in the shadows. "Daniel?"

"In the flesh." He studied his lover in concern. "You look like you've seen a ghost. Are you all right?"

"I am now." His shoulders relaxed, his smile wasn't the warmest Daniel had ever glimpsed. "I was merely concerned you might have been someone else."

"Who might that have been?" He bit his lip. He shouldn't be asking personal questions if he didn't want to be facing them himself one day but out it had popped, evidence his interest in his lover was more than a passing one. He was dying to know where he'd been all night.

Victor frowned. "An old friend, Viscount Hambly, startled me at dinner."

Curiosity burned yet again. "He was your last lover, wasn't he?"

Victor drew back a step. "Correct."

It was obvious from his clipped tone and change in posture Victor didn't like questions about his former affairs. Neither did Daniel, but he pressed on because he needed to know if he should bow out now before he got any further involved. Old loves were an unwanted complication. "And did you want to see him?"

"No." Victor's eyebrows rose high. "Why do you think my fists were raised?"

Relief slammed into him and he grinned foolishly. "Oh. It is very good to know you can defend yourself."

Victor shook his head. "That isn't really why you're smiling, is it?"

"Of course it is." He laughed. Victor was correct. He was absolutely delighted Hambly no longer had a place in the banker's affections. "A man should always have the means to do so."

His lover shrugged and removed his coat. Daniel moved to take it, breathing in Victor's calming scent.

The banker noticed his sniff and chuckled softly. "I'd hoped to see you at the club."

"Not tonight." An explanation bubbled up of why he hadn't dared show his face in public tonight, but he kept it behind his teeth, where all such explanations had to belong.

Victor nodded and loosened his neck cloth. "Can you stay long?"

Daniel moved Victor's hands aside and slowly removed the neck cloth himself. His cock thickened with arousal as he performed the small personal task for his lover, more so than he had for anyone else in a long time. "As long as you'll let me."

"As long as you like." Victor chuckled softly again.

"You're in an odd mood tonight." Daniel shifted closer and swept his hand around Victor's body. The banker leaned into his touch like a cat about to be scratched. Daniel knew just where to scratch too.

"Ready to beat me to a pulp first then laughing. What's so amusing to you?"

"I was asked almost the same question earlier tonight." Victor embraced him, nuzzling his throat and sending gooseflesh all over Daniel's body. "My responses were wildly different indeed."

"Did Hambly invite you to bed?"

Victor nodded slowly. "To an entertainment first, mostly for the fun of taking advantage of Lord Freeport's generosity as a host I'm afraid."

"That would be a mistake." Daniel met Victor's gaze in alarm. "Appearances can be an utterly wrong indicator of a man's true nature." That was all the warning he could give his lover. Despite his age and frequent appearance of befuddlement when out and about in society, Lord Freeport was not a man to cross.

Victor shrugged. "Well, I didn't say I wanted to go along. Hambly and I parted on bad terms a year ago, my decision actually, and his assumption that I will jump at the chance to take up with him again has grown to irritate me in the intervening hour since we spoke. I took a walk to cool my head, but it hasn't worked. He always was an arrogant arse. Most lords are, as you know. Very sure of your universal appeal. Hambly resented that I wouldn't give up my working hours to spend hours with him or share the particulars of my clients' finances."

"That would irritate me too. Some things simply cannot be given up in life." Daniel brought Victor deeper into his arms and stroked his hands firmly down the man's back, burrowing his fingers into the muscle and bone as he went. He gripped Victor's arse and kneaded the firm globes. He didn't like the direction this discussion was headed, discussing other men. He wanted to know what was going on at Victor's bank, but his tongue was tied by their arrangement. He could be an arrogant arse at times, but it had nothing to do with being an earl. He usually knew what he wanted. Learning about Victor's life, and that included his work, seemed the natural next step.

He kissed Victor swiftly and found comfort in that simple gesture. He was pleased to know, very pleased in fact, that it was well and truly over for Victor and Hambly. Some men could be difficult to end a relationship with.

Victor captured his face between his hands and planted a hearty kiss on his lips. "Enough of today. I want you naked and in bed with me."

That had been Daniel's plan too, originally. "I thought you'd never ask." Daniel laughed softly. "I do love the way we speak our minds to each other. It's very rare."

"I agree."

This time it was Victor who led Daniel into bed, removed their clothes, and arranged them comfortably so he was on top. They kissed deeply and it was Victor who grabbed the first cock. Then he slithered down the bed until his face was level with Daniel's groin and kissed his shaft. "I've been thinking of you all day."

Surely not *all* day. There'd been that matter in the bank Daniel couldn't ask about. He could still feel the tension in Victor's body, but he'd do his best to distract him thoroughly tonight. "You've been on my mind too."

Victor licked his cock and glanced up his body. "You came to see me today? What was that about?"

The handkerchief he'd meant to give as a token of his esteem was still in his jacket pocket, too far away to reach at the moment. He didn't want to move. "I was passing and just needed to see you."

Those soft blue eyes crinkled at the corners when Victor smiled. Excitement spun through his limbs. Daniel breathed in his lover's scent. He would definitely have to acquire a bar of that soap he washed in to take on his missions.

Victor lowered his face and nuzzled his balls. "What I like is how you are so obviously excited whenever you see me. You make me want to kiss you no matter who might be around."

A light nip of teeth on his balls had him gasping. "No pain."

The drag of a tongue across his balls next made him moan. "I won't hurt you. Not ever."

With the surety of a man who knew what he was about, Victor took his balls into his mouth and lavished them with hot wet suction. Daniel widened his legs as far as he could, giving up his pleasure to the man hovering now on his knees over him.

Victor had a gift. His mouth set Daniel's senses on fire. When he licked lower, headed for the crack of his arse, Daniel had to stifle a desperate groan. Having his bottom kissed, licked, was one of the most arousing gifts anyone could bestow on him. He liked it more than being fucked, though if Victor wanted him that way he'd never resist. But Victor had never tried to mount him. Not even suggested it once in the whole time of their involvement. "I must have been an idiot to wait so long for you."

The banker lightly nipped his inner thigh, urged Daniel's feet into the air, exposing his arse and making his intention to kiss it very plain. "We both were. Lie back and let me love you the way I want to."

He sucked in a quick breath as anticipation filled him with unbearable lightness. "By all means love me. I'm all yours."

Victor moaned then darted out his tongue to lick across his hole. Daniel closed his eyes and savored the sensations dominating his mind. The man had talent. Yes, indeed. Daniel would love to feel this way for the rest of his life if it were possible.

He stretched to touch Victor's head but could only intermittently graze his hair. When Victor stabbed his tongue deep into him, Daniel stroked his cock, his senses soaring.

"Wait," Victor demanded between kisses and licks.

Reluctantly, Daniel let his hand slide away to his leg and held on. Before long, his balls ached for release and he warned Victor he was close.

Victor lowered his feet to the bed, and then straddled his thighs, forcing his balls tightly together. Daniel's cock throbbed desperately between them, harder than he'd been in a long time. Seed ran in a long stream down from the tip. The banker grinned wickedly. "Did you eat oysters again?"

"No, it's how you affect me."

Victor's eyes glowed with warmth and affection. He rose to his knees and with a bit of maneuvering, sank onto his shaft.

Daniel gasped. "No oil?"

His lover rolled his hips, sinking deeper. "Can't wait."

Without oil to aid his passage, the sensations were very different. Victor was tighter, clinging firmly around his length, dragging on the soft skin of his cock with every movement. With the added friction Daniel didn't last beyond a moment.

His hips rose from the bed as he shot his seed deep and cried out his lover's name. Victor moaned as Daniel suddenly slipped more smoothly in and out. His speed increased while he used Daniel's own release to spur his along.

Daniel gripped the base of his cock, holding firm and straight as Victor fucked himself on the softening length. His thighs bunched and strained until he cried out too, shooting seed all over Daniel, splattering his chest and lips with the force of his release. He licked his lips. "Hmm, I needed dinner."

Victor lowered himself for a languid kiss and Daniel's cock slipped free. They groaned and then laughed as the rapidly cooling seed stuck to them both.

Daniel held Victor hard against him. "I could get used to this."

Victor nipped his jaw gently and wriggled. The seed on his chest coated them both and Daniel flipped Victor over to hold him still. He studied the man. "Damn, but you are a sexy one."

A flush of color grew on Victor's cheeks and he glanced down at Daniel's chest. His brow furrowed as he traced the fading scar across his chest. "How did you get this?"

Questions. "I was careless once too often."

The banker's touch was a light flare of sensation. "A blade did this?"

"Yes, just the tip scraped me," Daniel confessed after a moment. He didn't mention it to Victor, but if the strike had been any closer, or any harder, he might actually have been cleaved in two.

Victor wriggled and licked his seed from the edge of the scar with his talented tongue. He moved to the gunshot wound and stared. When he moved to kiss it too, Daniel cupped his head and held the man against him. Victor's reactions were not the same as his previous lovers had been. They had either been horrified or had poked at the wounds and attempted to pry information from him. So far, Victor seemed only concerned he'd been hurt.

A thought occurred to him. "How old are you?"

"Six and thirty," Victor replied, his response muffled by Daniel's skin as he licked the seed away.

"You're older than me by three years." He huffed at his mistake. "I would not have thought so."

Victor gently nipped his bicep. "How old did you think I was?"

"I don't know. Certainly not in your thirties."

His lover chucked. "Wealthy men, lords, don't give young upstart bankers their fortunes to manage."

"I suppose they don't." Daniel nudged Victor's legs wider apart and rubbed his softened cock into his lover's balls gently. "You wear your age well, my friend."

Victor met his gaze as he grabbed Daniel's wrist and held it up for closer inspection. "You hide your experiences better."

Again he gently kissed the wound, a burn that was still very rough, lavishing so much attention that Daniel was soon hard as a rock. They both were, if the pressure digging into his belly was any indication. Since they'd both already found one release, Daniel waited to see if Victor would take the lead and fuck him.

They kissed, deeply and with ample use of tongue and teeth, bodies restlessly straining against each other. After a while, Daniel was ready for more, but still Victor remained compliant beneath him. He'd have to ask now. "Do you like to fuck men?"

Victor met his gaze. "It's not something I'm compelled to do often. I'm sorry."

The way Victor timidly phrased his reply made Daniel's heart ache. Someone had had a problem with Victor's preference before if the man thought he needed to apologize. "So, you don't mind if I have you again?"

"No, please." Victor blinked. "Were you waiting to see if I wanted you first?"

"A bit." Daniel arranged Victor's legs wider apart for better access and settled the tip of his cock in place. "I thought it would be *arrogant* to assume I always could have you."

As he sank in, Victor tensed, stretching along the bed and pushing his head into the pillow. "I love being beneath a man. Beneath you is heaven."

Those words, and the manner of their confession, thrilled Daniel to his core. He set a slow rhythm, aiming to brush across the part of his lover inside that brought such sweet release when touched. Victor fisted his hands into the sheets and panted heavily. The sight was irresistible, etching itself indelibly on his memory. Victor was a man so clear and sure of his preferences that hopefully he could overlook Daniel's secretive nature and always welcome him.

With every fiber of his being he adored this man.

He loved Victor.

Daniel's thrusts faltered, and he balled his hands into fists on the mattress beside Victor's hips. Falling in love hadn't been his plan. When he met Victor's gaze he saw the same depth of emotion staring back, a little of his anxiety eased. He resumed his slow thrusts, keeping eye contact. When the man bit his lip and drew in a shuddering breath, Daniel did too. They were more in tune than he'd ever experienced. "Together?"

Victor gripped his forearms and wrapped his legs high around Daniel's back. "Yes, together."

Daniel opened his mouth to shout as his body suddenly clenched and shook. Victor beat him to crying out but only barely. Daniel collapsed and dragged Victor tightly against him. After a moment, Victor's strong arms wrapped around him and they held each other until the need to make love rose again.

CHAPTER SEVEN

Victor contentedly nestled against his pillows as Daniel climbed from his bed in the early hours of the morning. Sunlight warmed the earl's bare muscular back and the sight stirred him, even after hours of lovemaking. Their night together had been everything he'd needed and more. Tender and exciting. Daniel had made him feel completely desirable and his heart beat a little easier that what he'd offered in passion was enough for the other man.

Now that the morning was here, he faced the challenges of repairing the bank's reputation. Of finding out why he'd lost business in the first place. Despite the time he'd spent considering the matter, he was no closer to deciding how to go on with his investigations.

By daylight, the marks etched into Daniel's body were more apparent than they'd been at night and his heart ached anew. His lover had suffered a great deal over the years. Was more hurt to come for the secretive man? He sincerely hoped not because he didn't think he could bear losing him.

Thinking of Daniel's secret life gave Victor an idea, so he sat up, crossing his legs beneath him and fiddled with the sheet while he worked out how to phrase his question. He didn't want Daniel to think he was prying into his affairs, but a spy, and Victor was more certain by the moment that his lover was engaged in such dangerous activity, could put him on the right path to finding answers. "I'd like to ask you a question if I might," he said carefully, offering a tentative smile.

"That depends on what you want to know."

Better to be blunt. Daniel had said just last night he enjoyed his direct tendencies. "If you wanted to ruin someone's life how might a man go about it?" Now that the question was out in the open, Victor's skin crawled.

What would his lover think of his character after hearing that?

Daniel squinted as he ran his hand over the stubble darkening his jaw. "Is that a loaded question? Are you about to declare war on your competitors?"

Victor laughed, but it sounded strained so he tried to clarify his position without revealing why he needed to know. "I don't mean to ruin anyone, only know how it might be done and discreetly avoid anyone making an immediate connection to the perpetrator."

His lover pursed his full lips and returned to dressing with slow deliberate movements. He wrapped his cravat around his throat and tied it into a swift, neat knot. The corner of his mouth lifted with the beginnings of an amused smile. "How ruined where you proposing?"

"I'm not clear on the final outcome." Tension grew within him and fisted the sheet draped over his lap. "How would one begin?"

Cravat perfect, pin in place, Daniel pulled on his waistcoat and glanced down at the buttons as he replied, "Attacking a man's reputation would be the first step."

Victor nodded. He was already experiencing that now but he needed more information on what might come next. The earl appeared utterly unruffled by the conversation they were having and that went a long way to calming Victor's anxiety. "And then?"

Daniel drew on his trousers, tugged on his shoes and checked his reflection in the mirror. "That would depend on the end result I wanted."

"There are choices in these things?"

"There are choices to be found in everything." Daniel faced him, pulling on his coat and tugging his shirtsleeve cuffs into place. The only thing missing was some attention from a razor and he'd look perfectly turned out. No one would suspect he'd never made it home last night. "If I wanted revenge, to break my adversary and bring about the utter destruction of their life, I would take everything I knew they valued away from them. Family, friends, wealth, estate. The best revenge is when the pain is absolute and can be seen by all."

Victor gulped at that prospect.

"But if I were only out to prove a point, I'd settle for a lesser hurt. I'd take something valuable but not quite so vital to my adversary's life, or obvious to others when removed. Something they would miss but only in their quiet moments."

Victor eagerly leaned forward. "What might that entail if utter destruction wasn't my goal?"

"A wager to win a favored horse, theft of art of a particularly sentimental value. Something the person loved above all else. Even stealing away a lover has been tried many times before and often very successfully."

A business venture failed through loss of confidence by its customers.

Victor thought through the scenarios Daniels had suggested with that in mind. He had no family and few friends, but his business partner and Hawke's tenderhearted wife were both very dear to him. He couldn't bear it if Abigail and Hawke were hurt because he'd unwittingly offended someone to the point where they'd bring down such ruin on him. He would have to pay more attention to their life and make sure all was well with them before he did anything else.

The idea that someone might try to take Daniel away from him caused a small stir of unease too. He'd grown to love the man despite his secretive nature and the short duration of their association. However, Daniel had just proven he did know more than a little of the tactics used in revenge and could likely spot a nasty scheme before anyone tried it on him. If he was, in fact, a spy he would surely be able to smell the truth through any manure and take steps to protect their budding friendship. He seemed a man who made up his own mind. Just as Victor always did. They had one more thing in common.

Daniel frowned. "Does that help?"

"Yes," he promised, sitting back easily now he had his answers. "That is much more detail than I will ever likely need. Thank you."

"You're very welcome." Daniel came close and leaned

over the bed. He tugged at the sheet with a slow deliberate precision that made Victor's heart race. Despite the exertions of last night, his cock swelled as a wicked twinkle lightened Daniel's eyes. His lips parted and then lowered his head to Victor's groin. Full lips brushed over his cockhead in a soft kiss, and Victor moaned.

Daniel eased onto the bed slowly, never leaving off kissing Victor's cock. Dear God the man knew what he was about. Despite his need to get to work soon, he couldn't tell his lover to stop. The earl brought Victor's cock upright from where it curved against his belly and ran his tongue around the head several times. He tongued the slit, lapping up all the seed that had begun weeping from it.

Victor shuddered, completely caught up in the unexpected morning lust consuming him. He'd only ever had his own hand at this time of day. A moment later, his length was engulfed in the warmth of a hot mouth, his shaft lapped expertly by an experienced tongue before delicious suction began. He cupped Daniel's head, enjoying the occasional rasp of whisker along his shaft as his head rose and fell. He could watch the earl do anything most likely and become aroused, but this gift, this pleasure, was something else.

Daniel's attentions grew firmer and Victor closed his eyes tightly, focusing on what was being done to him. The earl stroked his cock with one hand, occasionally dove low enough to take him deep into his throat, and played with his balls. Victor's release built quickly. The touch of Daniel's fingers dipped and he swirled his finger around the skin between balls and arse, and then applied more pressure. Victor's hips rose. He drove his cock into Daniel's mouth as astonishing desire ripped through his body. He convulsed, shooting seed down Daniel's throat without warning. The tremors lasted awhile, affected him so strong that he took much longer than normal to open his eyes.

When he met Daniel's gaze, the man was grinning. "Now, that is just the way to start the morning, isn't it?"

Exhaustion weighted his limbs, but he returned the smile, wishing they didn't have to part that day. "I may never move again. Give me a moment to catch my breath and I will attend to you too."

"That was only for you to remember me by." Daniel kissed him soundly. "I had better go so you can get to the bank."

There wasn't the faintest hint of resentment in his words and Victor tenderly touched Daniel's whiskered jaw. How long would it be before the man left a razor next to his own? "I will see you when I see you."

Daniel's eyes twinkled as he smiled broadly. "As soon as I can, I promise."

They kissed again, deeply, then Daniel wrenched himself away with a wry chuckle. Victor understood. He didn't want to part from Daniel either. Everything they did together was wonderful. Victor wanted more of the same.

He watched his lover's broad back as he strode for the front door until he was out of sight. The outer door closed quietly after him, but his presence lingered, giving his apartment a homey atmosphere it had lacked before.

He chuckled softly to himself and climbed unsteadily to his feet. He did need to get moving or he would be very late. And he was never late for the work he loved. His body might be as sated and relaxed as never before, but his mind was invigorated by his life. Daniel in the morning, the pleasure of his work during the day, and more wicked play with his lover to look forward to later that night perhaps. He made his way to the bank with a lighter step and full heart, but still bound and determined to find out whom had the most to gain if his business went under.

CHAPTER EIGHT

Daniel let himself into the tiny sitting room Angelo Marinari used as his office as bawd of the Hunt Club. He'd been careful and not passed anyone of note on the way from Victor's apartment to the club. Keeping his hat low, and moving as if he'd every right to be there had always served him well. If he was lucky, he could be in and out of the club with none the wiser.

The Angel was dressed in female clothing as usual, quite an arresting sight and one that continued to fool many men, often until it was too late. A soft, blue silk that any woman would envy, and probably did, sealed the illusion. Marinari had the perfect figure for the day's light fashions. He didn't need to create more than a hint of false breast to present well in his current creation.

Marinari smiled when their eyes met. "You are early."

Daniel held a finger to his lips to ask for quiet. He slipped into the adjoining private bedchamber without speaking and began undressing. He'd long kept a razor here, and other items of clothing to change into if the need arose. He needed them now.

The other man rushed into the room after him, shut the door quietly. His wary glance proved Daniel had conveyed the right degree of alarm. "What's going on?"

There was no point beating about the bush. He wagged a finger. "You are late. They have noticed and I'm afraid I can't put them off much longer."

Marinari leaned against the door. "What will you do?"

"What will *we* do?" Daniel countered, digging through a drawer of Marinari's undergarments to find his razor. He quickly sharpened it with the strap Marinari kept behind the doorway and dealt with the task of making his face presentable. There was no point drawing any more attention to the fact he'd not gone home last night. He wasn't ashamed of being with Victor, the man drove him wild, but he did owe the man his discretion and protection. He also had to remain in hiding as long as possible. "We have to get you out of London. Possibly out of England altogether."

Silence greeted his announcement and he took the opportunity to retrieve his clothes from among Marinari's things. His clothing had been scattered amidst the feminine gowns, ensuring that it wasn't easy to spot them among the silk and muslins. When he'd changed and glanced away from the mirror Marinari was vigorously tossing his head from side to side, denying his request. "I am otherwise engaged."

"In a situation that leads to disappointment." He perched on the edge of Marinari's bed and stared at the reluctant assassin. "You must know that what you want isn't ever likely to come to pass."

Leaving the King's employ openly would only happen if Marinari was to die doing his duty, but Daniel was also speaking of the assassin's hopeless affection for Lord Bracknell, a married man with decidedly narrow views on passion. Despite a year of determined effort on Marinari's part, Lord Bracknell was no closer to succumbing to his very brazen offer to explore new experiences.

Marinari's eyes grew flat, hostile. "I've made my choice."

He approached the assassin and gently touched his shoulder. "I was followed after my last briefing. There is a price on your head, and likely on mine by now too."

Marinari's gaze shot to his. "How dare they."

"They do dare." Daniel shrugged. His anger had long since cooled thanks to Victor's calming influence. "Apparently, I'm no longer considered a trusted man, not that I blame them entirely. I *am* keeping your whereabouts from them."

The other man stepped away, his long skirts snapping with every movement. "They will regret not trusting you."

"When it comes to you, I've not been the least bit forthcoming." He pursed his lips. "Something has changed between my superiors that cause me concern. Freeport has always been a cagey devil, but I couldn't get the slightest hint whether I had his support or not."

He sighed. "Pickens, however, was openly hostile about you. He wants to see you immediately."

Marinari paused mid-step. "That was not our arrangement. Pickens is the new man, isn't he? I've not had the pleasure. Describe him. The name tugs on my memory."

"Not surprised you don't remember him. Spent ten years as an agent on the Continent, so he isn't immediately recognizable to many at first glance. Late fifties, balding, red-faced, and full of piss and wind. He's got this habit of tapping his fingers on the tabletop that drives one to distraction."

The assassin stiffened. "You must surrender to Lord Freeport immediately."

Surrender was never a term Marinari used lightly and Daniel's skin prickled. "Why?"

"I recall the name now. The man I knew as Pickens is already dead. I saw him put in the ground."

Daniel gripped Marinari's arms tightly. "When?"

Marinari lifted a hand to his brow. "Long ago. On the outskirts of Brussels, well before I ever came to England and became your King's puppet."

"He cannot be an imposter. He is well known to all in Society. He is invited everywhere."

"Believe me, a man does not recover from having a hole blown into his chest from cannon fire. The real agent is very dead, I assure you. The man you describe is a nervous one. Pickens had none of that about him. He was a killer and killers never have habits anyone would notice so easily."

Fear climbed Daniel's spine. Pickens's tapping fingers were in many pies. "Then who is this man really?"

"I don't know." Marinari bit his knuckle. "At a guess he must have replaced Pickens soon after my assignment without anyone discovering the switch. You must go to Freeport immediately. I will not have you harmed. I will follow after investigating this imposter and if required I will deal with the matter personally."

"I might not be believed if you are not with me."

Marinari pulled out the rosary he always carried about him and kissed it. "I swear. I will report to Freeport's home in person tonight, but only to him."

The only time Marinari ever revealed his grandmother's rosary was when it was a matter of life or death. That he swore on it now to prove his point was his promise to come or die in the attempt. It was a relief to Daniel that Marinari was keen to uncover this new threat. They had always made a good team when they worked together before. "How can I help you?"

"You cannot. Speed is vital. I will not be using sanctioned methods."

Daniel frowned, but Marinari broke away and ripped off his gloves. He raised his hands to his hair, unraveling the intricate pinning that helped convey a femininity he lacked. A damp cloth removed the coloring applied to his lips, but a smear stained the corner of his mouth.

Daniel lifted his hand and brushed the corner of Marinari's lips with his thumb. "You missed a spot."

"Thank you."

A sharp stab of pain pierced Daniel's chest. "So, this is it."

Marinari met his gaze. "Not quite. But it must be the last time. I will see it through to the end."

Daniel knew exactly what he meant. No matter what the outcome, The Angel would never follow orders again. He should not come back to the club either. He pulled Marinari into his arms and held him tightly, regretting he would lose a man who had become a trusted friend. "I will miss you, saucy minx."

Marinari's arms tightened around his waist, his face pressed against Daniel's chest like a lover would. They had never been more than friends, work colleagues in the beginning, but had pretended to be more often enough that the embrace was comforting rather than exciting. "Don't lie. If not for me, you'd have been free to have the life you were meant to have long ago. Once this is over, you can finally let someone get close to you."

"I may have found the man already." Daniel grinned

foolishly and kissed Marinari's silky dark hair. "You do realize you are the most sentimental assassin I've ever met."

"No one need know but us."

He patted Marinari's back. "I'm sorry it has to end this way."

The other man huddled a little closer and sniffed back tears. "I will miss you. I will miss this. You should go before I change my mind."

The door banged open noisily behind them. "What the hell is this?"

Marinari broke from his arms as Lord Bracknell strode into the room, caught Daniel by the cravat and threw him against the nearest wall like a rag doll. Given the force behind the action, and the throbbing in his head, Daniel wouldn't be surprised if the plaster hadn't cracked. Bracknell stood between Daniel and Marinari, chest heaving, eyes wild with fury. "What have you done?"

Daniel gingerly pressed against the back of his head checking for damage, taking note of Lord Bracknell's protective stance and Marinari's shocked expression. Apparently, the assassin had been gaining ground in Bracknell's affections and hadn't even realized it. Unexpected and unfortunate. "It's none of your business, Bracknell."

"It damn well is."

It was too late, of course. Once this mission was over The Angel would cease to exist. He could never reveal himself to Lord Bracknell ever again. Daniel glanced past Lord Bracknell and nodded to Marinari. "I am sorry. I will be waiting where we discussed."

Marinari stepped forward, his eyes pleading. "Can you wait a few hours?"

Daniel closed his eyes briefly. Marinari wanted one last chance to love Bracknell and who was he to deny him that one last kindness. It wasn't rational or wise, but he couldn't find the will to say no. "Very well."

Marinari nodded decisively, and the lingering liveliness that had erupted in his expression at Lord Bracknell's arrival changed to intent.

Daniel saw himself out quickly, ignoring the furious

whispers of the ladies and gentlemen lingering above stairs and feeling an absolute beast for grudgingly granting the little good Marinari had found in life. Circumstance and betrayal had made the man a killer. Efficient, lethal, uncompromising. He'd had no chance for any other life until he'd come to the club and what went on here wasn't normal or respectable.

Disgusted with himself, and with what must be done in the coming days, Daniel pondered his next move. He could not head directly to Lord Freeport's home to surrender himself; if he did he risked revealing Marinari's location should someone follow his trail in reverse. He needed to lay a false trail to give Marinari the time he needed. Daniel had to get out of the club in someone ordinary's company.

He sauntered into the dining room and glanced around to see who might suit his needs. Unfortunately, it appeared too early for many members to have arrived, so he requested whiskey with his breakfast while he planned what his false trail would entail.

Across the room, he spotted Lord Hambly, Victor's former lover, among a group of half a dozen pompous lords, watching him with hooded eyes. Since he wasn't particularly acquainted with any of them, he merely nodded, but he couldn't help the sense of discomfort that remained. From what he'd learned, Hambly hadn't been good for Victor, certainly not for his confidence, and for that reason alone Daniel couldn't use him.

Victor's unexpected early morning question returned to mind. What had he meant by asking how one might stage a revenge, and who did he wish to ruin? Vindictiveness didn't seem to be part of his makeup. Victor was an amiable man. Kind. In all of their acquaintance, he'd never heard a bad word spoken against the banker. He was scrupulous too. Daniel recalled his pale face and tension the evening before. Was Victor intending to ruin someone or was he the victim of such a scheme?

The latter did make more sense when Daniel considered the matter and Victor's obvious interest in revenge. His bank was remarkably successful. There was sure to be jealousy among those of his profession.

And in business it did not pay to be timid. At least here among the club's patrons, Victor would be treated fairly, spared of gossip about his proclivities that might harm his reputation in the outside world. The club's rules protected them all and for that Daniel would always be grateful to be a member. Here in the club, and at Victor's home, were the two places in London he felt most comfortable.

Across the way, he spied Mr. Joseph Mumford poised at the doorway to the dining room, appearing uncertain about whether to join the loud and laughing group or not. Another banker but one without the same flair, or was it ease, as Victor around the noble born.

He too carried a folio clutched to his chest. The man would be perfect for what Daniel had in mind, so he waved Mumford over to the seat across from him. There was good light, a side table to set his work upon, and Daniel wouldn't care if he barely spoke. As long as they could leave together, planting the assumption of them doing business together, he would be happy because no one would think twice about it.

Mr. Mumford hurried across the room and shook Daniel's hand firmly with a dry grip. "Good morning."

"It is," he lied. There was no point in burdening Mr. Mumford with his ruminations, so he put them from his mind.

Mr. Mumford requested coffee and a piece of seed cake from a footman then settled himself, albeit a trifle timidly, in the vacant chair. "I was surprised you'd want to associate with a fellow like me."

Daniel raised an eyebrow at his comment. Had he suddenly become high in the instep when he wasn't looking? "I speak to many men here. I detest snobbery of any form."

Last week Daniel had spent a few days as a stable hand, mucking out stalls at an inn while tracking the movements of several distinguished gentlemen. He was the last person to care about class and what one might have to do in his life.

"That is very kind of you to say." Mr. Mumford's smile was tentative at best and once he had his coffee and cake he devoted his attention almost exclusively to his papers. Daniel glanced the man's way as the occasional curse reached his ears. Mr. Mumford could take lessons from Victor on how to remain utterly inscrutable around others. It was very easy to see he was struggling with his calculations and that couldn't be good for his reputation.

He cleared his throat to make the banker stop. Mr. Mumford's head snapped up. Daniel smiled warmly. "I'm sorry to disturb, but you seem a trifle vexed."

Mumford sighed. "It isn't fair. I can calculate the profit for my clients as easily as I breathe, but taking an accounting of my mother's finances is beyond me today. It is much like deciphering ancient Egyptian hieroglyphs."

"Oh." Daniel laughed, relieved his concerns were for naught. "I am lucky and leave that sort of reckoning to my brother. He knows better than to torture me with facts and illegible figures."

"It must be nice to have someone to rely on. I have only myself and at times..." Mumford left the rest unsaid

Daniel could easily fill in the gaps. At times it was a struggle. He was certain Victor must feel the same sort of pressure to bring his clients a profit. But Victor had Mr. Hawke to rely upon and to talk to about their business. "Do you have a partner in your business, sir?"

"Not as yet but perhaps one day soon." Mumford touched his nose and winked. He checked the time on his pocket watch and rushed to put his papers away. "I have an appointment here in a few moments. Thank you so much for your company. Do excuse me."

"Of course."

The man sprang to his feet and moved toward the saloon. Daniel groaned. Accompanying Mumford to his place of business could have been a perfect false trail. A pity he'd needed to see a client and here of all places. From this position, Daniel had a clear view into the corner Mumford had relocated in. After a few minutes had passed, Lord Hambly joined the banker and the viscount's greeting was remarkably effusive. Daniel was surprised at that. From what he'd noticed of Hambly, he didn't seem the type to show interest in anyone without a title too openly. Not even with Victor around the club and Daniel suspected they'd been meeting here for a year or so at the time of their affair. Mumford and Hambly soon had their heads together over more papers and Daniel looked away.

What would Victor think about that relationship? Would he care his former lover was flirting with another banker.

Daniel sighed. His heart wasn't truly suited to inactivity if he was speculating on other men's love affairs. He pushed to his feet, had a hack called and after a long winding trip around London alone, he headed for Lord Freeport's home.

He hoped when this call was completed he might still have time and liberty to see Victor tonight.

CHAPTER NINE

Victor showed Mr. Davis to the door with a pleased smile. Davis had come to question his accounts too but now hinted he might increase his investments through them instead. A fellow member of the club, Victor had had no hesitation in laying out the findings of the auditors who had inspected their business dealings from top to bottom and side to side.

Mr. Davis' stunned expression had been reassuring. Victor had pressed to know the source of his earlier unease. The fellow had been tight lipped as to that, but Victor could tell by the frequent reassurances that he would do his own investigation.

It must be a rumor and spread rather carefully.

He closed the door to his office and grinned. Having the man on his side, assured of his sincerity and competence, would turn things around in his favor again. He reviewed the notes he'd made from previous visits. The man had invested a tidy sum with him, but also utilized the services of other bankers to increase his fortune.

Victor approved of diversification of interests and had no cause for concern until he remembered one of Mr. Davis' other bankers was Mr. Mumford—a young man at the beginning of his career, and a nephew.

He reviewed his notes in closer detail. Davis was cautious to a fault. Mumford had only been given a token sum to invest until he'd proven himself to his uncle. The man *had* done well with those funds, according to Mr. Davis today. *Interesting.* A young man on the verge of his career could be very ambitious. Would he stoop to a smear campaign in the hope of attracting new clients? Victor wasn't sure about him, but he knew others who had behaved in such a manner before. Mr. Mumford would bear closer investigation if the rumors afflicting his business did not cease.

A clerk tapped on his door. "You have a visitor."

Ordinarily, the clerk would announce his caller by name, especially if it was an existing client, so he was rather intrigued when the young man grinned excitedly. "By all means send them in." He stood and was surprised to see Mrs. Hawke tumbling into his room, giggling a little as her husband followed her in.

"We wanted you to be the first to know," Abigail Hawke gushed breathlessly.

Victor set his papers aside. "Know what?"

His staff lingered just at the doorway behind the Hawkes, attempting to listen in.

His partner closed the door in their faces then wrapped his arms about his wife. "We have good news."

Abigail blushed. "We are to have a baby by winter."

Victor grinned and flung himself around the desk. He hadn't been expecting such an announcement yet, but he was very pleased for his partner and wife. He kissed Abigail's hot, blushing cheeks, shook hands with Hawke and stood back to take in their happiness. "By winter. What an efficient pair you are."

Hawke and Abigail hadn't been married very long. By the time the babe came it would only just be their second wedding anniversary.

Hawke twirled his wife around and they laughed and kissed despite Victor's presence. Marriage had been just the thing for David Hawke. The man had never been happier. He would make a wonderful father. He would take his child to Brighton and spoil him with the childhood he'd had—running wild on the seashore.

The reality of that future soon took the gloss off Victor's joy. Hawke would need more time away from the business to spend with his young family. Victor couldn't expect him to be here at all hours as he was now. He kept his concerns to himself, but how he would bear the extra responsibilities without giving up socializing altogether? Would Daniel grow sick of his long hours and eventually drift away, leaving Victor to find pleasure with his toys? He didn't want that.

But he couldn't run Hawke and Knight Bank almost by himself.

For the first time in his life Victor considered if he

could bear to sell the bank so he didn't have to lose his private life and a lover. He'd had offers to buy the business before but had never once considered them seriously.

Perhaps it was time.

Daniel stood as Lord Freeport entered his study, his steps unhurried across the parquetry floor of his home. He had been kept waiting a half hour already, and his nerves were not entirely settled. Although he counted it a blessing he'd been largely left to his own devices here in the private room, he didn't believe his luck would last.

"Lord Beecroft. What an unexpected pleasure." Freeport turned for the sideboard. "Sherry?"

"Yes, thank you." Although Daniel strained his ears, he could detect no other sounds within the house since he'd been sequestered here. Freeport had a wife and daughter who were not particularly quiet women and he thought he'd spotted them in Town just two days ago. Where were they tonight?

"What brings you to me?"

"Our mutual friend suggested I come forthwith," Daniel murmured quietly as he took the offered glass and brought it to his lips. He did not sip the liquid. The action was just for show.

"Our mutual friend has a touch of the sight about him," Freeport muttered, throwing a scowl toward the window.

"I would say concerned for all involved."

Freeport grimaced. "My wife and daughter will be sorry to have missed you. They are from Town visiting an old, dear friend from my wife's school days."

Daniel closed his eyes briefly in understanding. Freeport had sent his family away. "I am sorry to have missed them. Your wife has long been a favorite of mine."

"Yes, my wife speaks fondly of you too. It is her fondest wish to have you sweep my daughter off her feet for the altar."

Freeport's daughter was very lovely and many a lord had tried to saddle him with their daughters for a wife that he would normally ignore the suggestion. However, Freeport had never spoken of it before. He *had* claimed, time and again, that wives and spying did not mix well.

Daniel leaned forward. "Have you ever seen what cannonball fire can do to a man's chest? Quite a ghastly mess and an impossible injury to recover from."

Freeport started at his statement, a sign of alarm he couldn't dismiss. "Is that so?"

"Oh, yes." Daniel glanced around the room discreetly.

Freeport tossed back the contents of his glass and crossed to a sash window. He fiddled with the lock and then lifted the pane high to let in the night air. Next, he sat at his desk, opened the drawer and withdrew a pistol with a shrug. "These are troubled times."

Daniel sat up straighter, eying the weapon. He did not dare glance toward the door behind him as his scalp prickled with the awareness. His experience was too great to ignore the sensation that someone was watching him from the shadows beyond the door. "I agree."

"Difficult to know who to trust."

Daniel stared at Freeport hard. What was the man trying to say? Was he in danger? Were they both in peril tonight? The man was too bloody inscrutable for Daniel's comfort. If he was about to die he'd really rather it be quick than discuss it all night. The Angel was coming.

The Angel was walking into a trap.

He risked a peek at the window and darkness beyond. There, a pair of coal black eyes peeked from the shadows. The Angel was here already, and Freeport likely knew it. Daniel set his glass aside, unfinished, and as he sat back, he loosened the sheath housing his short blade hidden in his coat sleeve. He twisted his forearm and the blade handle slipped into his palm. He kept the blade hidden from view and stretched his senses. Was that a creak of floorboard beneath the stealthy approach of someone else? "I've always known who to trust."

A brief smile quirked the corner of Freeport's mouth. "You're a good lad."

"I try to be."

The Angel bounced through the window, landing

lightly on the balls of his feet dressed as a man for a change. "Get down!" he shouted to Lord Freeport.

Daniel dove sideways even as he sighted Lord Pickens framed in the doorway, pistol raised at The Angel. He fired just before Daniel flung his blade.

For a long suspended moment, Lord Pickens remained on his feet—a dark bloody hole in his forehead, Daniel's blade lodged in his shoulder. When he toppled backward, Daniel shuddered. He glanced around the room, quickly assessing the aftermath.

Lord Freeport remained on his feet, pistol in hand, and clearly in good health.

The Angel lingered by the window, but he threw a pouch onto the desk and then toppled backward through the opening.

Thinking him hurt, Daniel rushed for the window, vaulted out only to find himself entirely alone in the quiet garden. The Angel had vanished like mist. He thoroughly checked the area but found no sign of the assassin. Eventually, he climbed back through the window to face Freeport.

No doubt drawn by the noise of the pistol shot, Freeport was surrounded by his servants as they inspected the body. Eventually, the three caught Pickens by his arms and legs, and burdened by the heavy weight, shuffled from the room.

Freeport slapped Daniel's shoulder several times. "I do thank you." The older man moved to the sideboard and poured a glass of sherry, drank it in one gulp, then poured another. "Help yourself."

Daniel declined. "What's going on?"

Freeport scooped up the pouch The Angel had left behind and shook out the contents. A small journal, several papers, and a seal. He grinned and held up the seal. "We had a traitor in our midst. I needed this. Do give my compliments to our friend at the first opportunity. His assistance has again proven his skills at tracking down unpleasant individuals."

"So, should I expect to be followed again?"

Freeport's eyes narrowed. "That was never done on my orders."

"Ah," Daniel burned with curiosity but wisely held his

tongue. There was only so much he needed to know in his line of work. Sometimes, the less he knew the better. Since Freeport was reading his way through the contents of the pouch he stood, quite ready to be on his way. "If that is all?"

"Wait." Freeport held up a hand. He bit his lip a moment then lifted his gaze from the papers. "Tonight you are for Brighton. If I am reading this correctly, there is a rendezvous planned for tomorrow night that must be stopped at all costs. Take my men and our mutual friend. You will have need of his special skills to get the job done."

Daniel cursed under his breath. "Who are we to stop?"

"Pickens, or whoever that man was, had a manservant. You must intercept a Mr. Grendier, the imposter's valet, and collect his correspondence. I don't wish to see the body."

"Anything else?"

"Yes," Freeport said slowly. "This man pretending to be Pickens only managed the feat because of The Angel's activities in the past. That fellow assumed a position that had access to a great many influential assets and it must not happen again. This is the third one in as many years. In light of that, we feel the Angel has outlived his usefulness."

Daniel blinked in shock. "He saved your life tonight."

"He killed one of us too. We didn't know that before the bargain was struck. The life of every man who serves the Crown is continually put in jeopardy because of his past actions. Let me know that it's done on your return."

Daniel swallowed the fury building inside his chest. He couldn't ignore a direct command from Lord Freeport. He had the King's ear, and the Regent's trust.

Yet, in a fight against The Angel, Daniel might not survive. Marinari would fight hard for his life.

CHAPTER TEN

Daniel strode into the Hunt Club and scanned the crowd for Victor, even as he made his way toward Marinari's office late that evening. He had called at the bank and found it closed far earlier than normal. Then he'd gone to Victor's apartment, knocked and received no answer. He'd picked the lock and slipped upstairs to check that his lover hadn't been so absorbed in his work he'd missed hearing his knock at all.

He'd waited as long as he'd dared and to pass the time he'd done something that might get him into trouble—he'd completed Victor's unpacking.

Despite the urgency of his new mission, he couldn't bear to leave the apartment as it was. And he'd enjoyed arranging his lover's possessions in a better manner, finding many an interesting book or painting he'd like to learn more about. He hoped to return to ask those questions one day, but he wasn't counting on it. By the time he'd left, Victor's home at last appeared as if someone had actually lived there as long as the banker had. All that was needed was some food to fill in his empty cupboards and it would be a home to be proud of.

As he passed the dining room doorway, he heard laughter and his eyes were drawn to the source. Victor was sitting at a dinner table.

Relief slammed through him and he hurried in that direction. But he jerked to a halt a short distance away as Lord Hambly joined Victor. The man was smiling openly at his lover in a way that concerned him. They seemed cozy, set apart from all others. Uncertainty filled him. They were at a table for two, with no space for a third to join them. Much like Hambly's conversation with Mumford earlier in the day, their discussion seemed rather too intimate for him to blunder into.

Maybe he shouldn't interrupt.

Unfortunately, Victor turned his head at that moment and when their eyes connected the banker didn't smile. Hambly spoke and Victor's expression hardened.

What the hell was going on? Since tonight he'd have to leave London, perhaps never to be seen again, he crossed the room to speak to Victor. "Hello."

"Lord Beecroft," Victor replied in a flat, disinterested voice that cut Daniel to the quick.

"Do excuse me." Hambly stood, smoothing his waistcoat and preening in a manner Daniel found uncomfortable. "There's someone I must see. Until later, Victor."

Daniel didn't care for the way Hambly alluded to a later or for the light touch to Victor's shoulder that brought out all his usually well-buried possessive tendencies. He perched on the chair opposite Victor, his stomach twisting into knots. Victor's blue eyes were cold when their gazes met. Years of training helped Daniel hide his uncertainty, but it wasn't easy given his reception. "You finished work early today."

"I received some good news and rewarded everyone."

Did that mean his troubles at the bank, whatever they might have been, were over? Given the way Victor regarded him with such hostility, he didn't dare ask what that good news might have been. He nodded instead. "Excellent."

Victor reached for his wine glass, his mouth thinning momentarily before he drained it. As he lowered the glass, Daniel couldn't miss that his lover's hand shook the tiniest bit.

"Is something the matter?"

The banker pursed his lips. "You've had a busy day?"

Daniel had had an awful day and had been hoping seeing Victor would be the bright spark he needed to shake off the gloom before he left Town. "How so?"

Victor leaned forward. "It is bad enough you're in league with my competitor and meeting where anyone can see, but to turn to another mere hours after leaving my bed is an insult not to be borne."

Daniel gaped. "What makes you believe I was with someone else?"

"The news is all over the club about your altercation with Lord Bracknell over that trollop Marinari. Explain yourself."

Daniel clamped his lips shut over a protest. He could never explain himself to anyone's satisfaction and certainly not about Marinari. This had always been a sticking point with his lovers. His inability to share the small details of his life, his propensity to keep private his conversations with others secret, inevitably caused a wedge that no amount of silent pleading for understanding could ever overcome.

"My brother handles the estate management in my stead. He handles as much of my affairs as he is able. I trust him implicitly. I don't concern myself with money and have no need for a banker to advise me and if I did I would certainly not meet with them in the club. Everyone here gossips. If I had a need I would have asked you first."

Victor's jaw clenched. "I am not a fool."

Daniel bowed his head a moment. Marinari was the cause of Victor's anger but what could he say? Nothing unfortunately. Bracknell *had* been jealous and caused a scene. "I know you are not. You are the most dedicated, clever and forthright man of my acquaintance. I admire your business savvy and hope your love of your work gives you as much satisfaction as it seems it does."

His lover's mouth gaped at his compliments.

"You know my views on questions I cannot answer and I know you hold similar views. I had hoped you could trust in me, trust that my respect for you knows no bounds. I do not have the leisure to educate you. Shall we part ways now to spare us both further disappointments or can you give me the benefit of the doubt?"

Victor swallowed. "I think you should go."

Daniel's chest hollowed of all feeling and all he could do was nod slowly. Breaking with Victor now might just be the right decision given his current mission, but it still hurt. When he went on assignment he never knew if he would be coming back. That was why his brother managed his responsibilities. That was why he'd accepted his love affairs as short-term arrangements. Until today that had seemed almost easy. There would be no Victor waiting on him and wondering where he'd gone if this mission ended badly.

It was probably for the best.

He stood a little unsteadily and looked down upon Victor one last time. Pain grew until he understood what he'd lost. The most vital and important relationship he'd ever experienced. He'd lost the man he'd loved to the depths of his soul.

Victor met his gaze, his jaw set in a stubborn line and Daniel smiled sadly. Despite the unfairness, he couldn't regret one moment he'd spent with the banker. "Farewell, Mr. Knight. I wish you well. I wish you success, but before I go I wish to make one thing very clear."

Victor frowned. "Can you?"

"Hmm," he murmured. "In this I can. You should know that I've fallen in love you. Goodbye, Mr. Knight and God bless." He strode for Marinari's rooms quickly, lest he lose his pride and beg Victor to give him another chance. To wait. Victor did not call him back and he ignored the speculative glances that followed him through the club. *Damn meddling bunch of old women.*

Because of them he'd lost Victor and now there was no time to correct the situation. In fact, the situation would actually help him get out of the club and London with a valid explanation for his disappearance. It wasn't fair.

Marinari was waiting, utterly feminine to the ignorant eye once more. "And?"

He swallowed. "Take my arm, sweetheart."

Irritation filled Marinari's eyes. "Even after everything."

"Yes, I am sorry." He smiled sadly. "The affair is not over. This must be done and publically. Are you by chance wearing breeches under there?"

"Yes."

"Then there is no point in delay. We are required in Brighton forthwith." Marinari's shoulders slumped, but he took Daniel's offered arm after a moment. "Better pretend to be madly in love me," he whispered in the assassin's ear, earning a pinch in return.

They were both well aware that while they could act out any role with aplomb, their hearts belonged elsewhere.

Together, they strolled arm-in-arm through the club. Every eye followed them. To others it would look like the beginning of a grand love affair between them, but it was the end for Daniel. He felt rather than saw Victor's gaze upon him as they passed by the dining room doorway and he gritted his teeth instead of succumbing to melancholy and looking his way one last time.

This would work if he willed it to.

The night air was cool on the street and he drew Marinari nearer his side as he would a lady of the night. He hailed a hack, directed it to a small estate on the outskirts of Town where he occasionally pretended to meet lovers but in truth only kept a pair of horses and supplies for situations like this. Once the animals were saddled, he and Marinari turned their back on London as if the very devil chased them.

CHAPTER ELEVEN

Victor couldn't concentrate. He'd been staring at the same pages for the last hour and made no progress with his work. It was unlike him to find no comfort in his business affairs, but he was utterly useless for anything except thinking of his confrontation with Daniel last night.

He threw his pen across the desk then covered his face. In truth he was more disturbed by losing Daniel to Marinari than losing thousands in invested funds to another firm.

He was heartbroken.

Such a deep emotional connection to a lover had never happened to him before, or so quickly. Daniel's parting last night troubled him. He hadn't been able to sleep. Daniel had claimed to love him, yet the image of Daniel prancing from the club with Marinari, a woman, clinging to his arm so clearly full of love, filled him with anger and indescribable hurt.

He had hoped work would be a balm for his confusion, but he could barely keep still. How dare Daniel leave him for a woman? It didn't make the least bit of sense. Learning his lover had fought over Marinari's favors that morning with Lord Bracknell had been a blow to his pride, watching them leave the club together, arm in arm, had destroyed him.

For the first time in his well-ordered life he felt utterly out of control.

Hawke slipped into the room and shut the door firmly behind him. "You shouldn't be here."

Victor grimaced. "We have so much more to accomplish."

"Not today." Hawke leaned against the door. "I've never seen you so restless. I can hear you from my office and that is no small matter."

Victor could not explain. The intimate facets of his

personal life were none of Hawke's concern. He would not understand Victor was grieving the loss of another man. "I should be here," he affirmed, but his words lacked his usual absolute conviction even to him.

"I have a suspicion of what's wrong with you." Hawke pursed his lips. "We've never talked very much about our lives beyond the business. Since Abigail became part of my life, I've learned that bottling up emotions isn't very healthy. You can tell me anything. I'd never gossip and I wont *judge*."

Victor's breath caught. Did Hawke know about his preference for men? He'd never hinted he did, but the way his business partner stressed his words led him to think he'd not been as circumspect as he'd hoped. Victor chose his next words with care. "I met someone."

"I'd hoped so." Hawke smiled broadly. "New love can be confusing and it is daunting to let someone close enough to understand our insecurities."

That was true. He and Daniel kept their worlds separate. "I don't know what to do."

"Have you argued?"

"Not exactly. I argued and earned silence in return."

"The one you love is timid?"

"Not exactly, but very guarded. I fear I've lost to another."

Hawke's eyebrows shot upward. "You don't know for sure, do you? No wonder you are so out of sorts. That's not like you. I've always admired your propensity for facts above idle speculation."

"That speculation is founded on reliable intelligence from trusted sources and from my own view." The patrons at the club had talked of nothing but Lord Bracknell's outburst. Fighting in the club just wasn't done. And he had seen Daniel take Mrs. Marinari away with his own eyes. It wasn't hard to conclude what would come next.

"You know what you should do," Hawke said with his usual bold confidence. "Sort this out once and for all. Leave nothing undiscussed, your feelings, your love of work, so there can be no misunderstandings or further foolishness."

That would be sensible but...he'd never called on

Daniel outside the club. The man was an earl. What might he think of a lover confronting him at his own home? "I am not sure I will have the chance to do that."

"This came for you by the way." Hawke tossed a tiny package onto the desk then moved to the door and gripped the handle. "Listen. There's been a bounce to your stride these last few days that hasn't been there in years. Don't let the one you want get away because you quarreled over a potential misunderstanding. Sort it out."

He breathed a sigh of relief. Hawke had no idea about his preference for men after all. He eyed the package on the desk warily, perfectly wrapped package with a little string bow tied around it hardly ever were delivered to him. He hadn't the faintest idea what it could be. With his mind half on the task and half on Daniel, he untied the bow and discovered a note and a scrap of linen inside.

Dear Victor, a token of my sincere affection. Thank you. Warmest regards, Daniel.

Victor turned the linen over in his hands, puzzled by the unexpected item. He unfolded it and discovered a snowy white pocket-handkerchief, embroidered with his own initial. He slumped into his chair in confusion. What did Daniel think he was doing by sending gifts? One gave gifts to someone one cared for not for someone one cheated on.

Then that matter of Daniel's intimate tête-à-tête with Mr. Mumford, a man who clearly had ambitions to acquire new clients and grow his business, grated still. Hambly had said they were very friendly earlier in the day and were laughing over Mumford's papers. Clearly financial ones since they'd come from Mumford's folio as Hambly had found out when the man had approached him afterward.

Victor had no proof that Mumford was out to ruin him, but making friends with his current lover and a former one was rather hard to dismiss as merely a coincidence. He felt foolish for not having suspected he was being toyed with, but what did he know of deception. He was a man who preferred direct action and honesty.

Daniel's suggestion of loving him was likely a desperate ploy to manipulate him too. Hambly had always claimed to love him when they argued too, but he'd never said so publicly. Not as Daniel had done last night, so loud that others might have heard. Hambly had always said it in private as an attempt to make Victor change his mind. Daniel hadn't really tried. Just stated it as a fact and said goodnight.

No.

No, he hadn't said goodnight. "He'd said goodbye as if it was final."

Victor rubbed his brow as his head ached. Should he have pushed for the truth then and there? Forced Daniel to explain the circumstances of the altercation with Bracknell? What if it hadn't been a lover's tiff as everyone suggested?

He ran a thumb over the handkerchief's lettering. The embroidered V set his heart thumping because it was clearly a recent purchase. A sweet gesture. A very Daniel gesture. He set it aside, unsure what to make of the gift. Perhaps he should do as Hawke suggested and clear things up with Daniel today. He glanced down at his clothing. Home first to change and then he'd find out the truth himself.

He would not allow Daniel to get away without providing an explanation one minute longer than necessary.

CHAPTER TWELVE

The sea breeze whipped at Daniel's borrowed cloak and he pulled the thin garment tighter about him. "There it is."

Marinari followed his direction to stare across the water with dead eyes. From the moment they'd left London, he had been silent and sullen. Daniel could not blame him for his pout. He was unhappy too. Freeport's timing had been off by three days and their prey, Grendier, had remained idle in a Brighton tavern until now. But at last a small rowboat struggled toward the coastline and the little smugglers cove some miles south of the nearest town. Grendier paced the shore, waiting to meet it.

Knowing the job would soon be over was both a blessing and a curse. A blessing because Daniel yearned for London as well as Victor and a curse because he must return alone.

He gestured to the men supplied to him by Freeport—rough sorts who were paid well to kill without questions. "Spread out among the trees and stay out of sight until we have need of you. The Angel and I will deal with this quickly and quietly as ordered."

Instructions should have been unnecessary but these were Lord Freeport's sharp-eyed men and he suspected they too had orders where The Angel was concerned. They were not so quick to obey him and move away. If Marinari suspected he was in danger of being set upon at any moment, he gave no indication.

The assassin drew close and pointed along the shore. "There, see that slight depression? There is a ravine that runs all the way up the slope. He'll go that way to avoid detection after the trade is made."

Daniel nodded. It was also a perfect place to hide a body or two and no one would notice unless they stumbled directly into the ravine or came to investigate the odor of a rotting corpse. They picked their way ahead very quietly and stopped as close to Grendier as they dared.

The target the rowboat was headed for was quite deep near land. It would need to come almost completely to a stop beside the shoreline to carry out any exchange. Grendier wouldn't stand a chance of getting away unless he jumped in the boat or could swim.

Daniel turned to Marinari. "Give me your pistols."

Marinari held them out without question and Daniel tucked them into his pockets. The Angel usually fought hand-to-hand, favoring skill and silence over the noise of barking irons. He was a dangerous man but trusted Daniel. Daniel hoped he would prove worthy of that trust tonight.

They crept closer, confident the shadows hid their presence from those upon the water. When they reached the shoreline, the creak and splash of oars carried clearly across the water.

When Marinari hesitated, Daniel stepped forward to take his place.

Ahead, a man greeted Grendier but wobbled as he fought for footing on the precarious landfall. A satchel secured across his chest passed to Grendier and the exchange was made.

Traitor.

Since Daniel had no instructions for the men on the boat, he kept an eye on Grendier most of all. The rowboat put back to sea with a helpful shove from Grendier and the man stood a moment watching his conspirators leave. Once they were well away, he dusted off his hands and strode toward the ravine as Marinari had anticipated he would.

Daniel leaped into action, catching Grendier easily, jerking him 'round and snapping his neck before the man realized he had been caught red-handed betraying his King and country. The body crumpled to the ground, vacant eyes staring up at the night sky.

Now that Grendier was dead, Marinari had no further reservations about the mission and moved forward. Dead was dead, and Marinari's conscience was clean of this latest murder. He retrieved the evidence secured in the satchel, checked the dead fellow's clothing for anything else of value, and then handed it all to Daniel. "Not much of a spy."

Lord Freeport's men materialized around them, forming a half-circle with the water as a barrier along one side. Daniel had told them to stay back, but clearly now they were following other orders than the ones he'd given.

He judged their mood as determined. "A job well done," Daniel said, more for the benefit of Lord Freeport's men than his own conviction. He did not like it, but his orders concerning The Angel were as clear as the ones to dispose of the late Mr. Grendier on this mission. "Get him underground and quickly," Daniel ordered quietly to the nearest Freeport man. They couldn't remain here long. This wasn't the place men could meet without being held in the highest suspicion.

A shovel appeared and two fellows dragged the body away. More than half the men remained, all eyes trained on The Angel.

When the men came back too quickly for a careful burial to have been performed, Daniel took the shovel from one and sank the tip into the ground with a harsh shove. "Be on your way now. I'll report to Lord Freeport as soon as I return to London."

The Angel frowned as the men lingered, revealing all manner of weapons that had been concealed until now. The assassin was utterly outnumbered.

Finally alert to the danger he was in, The Angel took a fighting stance. Sadly, one without any weapons. Daniel even had the pistol Marinari carried that didn't shoot where aimed. It always pulled to the right by a wide margin but the assassin claimed he enjoyed the challenge of hitting any target with it.

In hand-to-hand combat, Daniel would last barely a minute against Marinari. Against ten men? They might last two. It wasn't necessary for these fellows to die following an order akin to suicide.

Thinking quickly, he withdrew The Angel's contrary pistol and aimed it at the assassin. He hoped to God the man recognized his own weapon and played along.

Marinari backed to the water's edge. "What are you doing with that?"

Daniel waved the pistol about so The Angel would pay even more attention to the weapon. Thankfully, his eyebrows lifted the tiniest amounts conveying his recognition.

Tricked into assurance of real intent, Lord Freeport's men backed away silently and Daniel thanked the stars because he wasn't sure this would work out well for anyone. "You know you have to die, don't you? You're too much of a risk. This is the only way."

A cloud covered the moon, but Daniel was close enough that he could easily make out Marinari's outline, framed as it was by the shimmering water behind him. He couldn't delay. It might be a farce, but their play had to be realistic.

"I cannot forgive this," The Angel hissed. "You bastard."

He sent up a quick prayer, aimed for Marinari's heart, and fired.

Marinari flew back into the water with a huge splash and he flailed around, gasping in shock only to go under again very quickly. The fire of the pistol brought Lord Freeport's men back to the shore. They stared at the water where the ripples of Marinari's descent into the cold depths confirmed his location. They remained there as bubbles rose.

Not one man volunteered to dive in to retrieve the body. Daniel counted that as a blessing. He turned away and strode back toward the horses as if he was unmoved by his actions. However, his heart was lurching in fear and guilt. What if he'd actually hit Marinari? What if he did drown?

Freeport's men hurried after him in the dark. He breathed a sigh of relief when a quick glance confirmed they were all accounted for and were mounting their horses.

The Angel would be dead now to everyone who needed to believe it. If he survived his dunking, he was on his own. A free man at last.

CHAPTER THIRTEEN

Victor shifted in his chair for the hundredth time, his gaze fixed on the club's entrance as another set of members wandered in. He was waiting for Daniel, but the man had eluded him. A spy would. Victor wished Daniel wasn't quite so good at his job.

He rubbed his tired eyes. He hadn't slept well for days, not since he'd discovered Daniel wasn't willing to see him and Marinari had deserted her position in the club too.

The club was in an uproar as a result.

He'd called at Daniel's home last night and again this morning only to be told, rather rudely in his opinion, that if he returned, the Watch would be called.

Victor was plagued with the suspicion Daniel had gone away from London entirely. When he'd stood on the footpath below Daniel's London Townhouse he'd not seen any lights in the upstairs windows. If only he possessed Daniel's knack of picking locks he could have slipped inside to determine if the man was actually away or merely avoiding seeing him.

Perhaps he was worrying over nothing but a sense of dread would not be silenced.

He had excused himself from business again today, which wasn't like him in the least. But until he saw Daniel, got a few things off his chest, his mind was not fit to concentrate on anything. Not on clients, not on investments, not on anything but the suspicion he might have been wrong in the first place.

He frowned as Mr. Davis barreled past the major domo without discarding his hat, his steps rushed, his face set in serious lines. His client hurried toward the offices of the Hunt Club with a determined stride, much resembling a duck's waddle when being chased.

Victor bit his lip at his imagination. Too little sleep and he was not making the least bit of sense even to himself. Daniel had a lot to answer for when he got his hands on him.

Mr. Mumford came in next and froze when their gazes met. A doe caught in a hunter's line of sight if ever there was one. Eventually, Mr. Mumford tipped his hat and quickly followed the path his uncle had taken a few moments earlier. Victor shrugged off a suspicion that something was going on and returned his gaze to the door just as Lord Hambly entered the club. He was relieved for the distraction even if it was Hambly.

The viscount rushed over. "There you are, Vicky. I called on you at home, but you'd left dashed early. Are you working here today?"

Victor checked the door again wishing the man he wanted to talk to most would hurry up and get his arse to the club. "No."

"My word, you look utterly spent." Hambly peered into his face. "I have just the thing to distract you. We could get a room or perhaps spend a day at your abode. I'm still waiting on an invitation to view your new living arrangements."

The man would be waiting awhile. When Victor was at home, he couldn't help but think of Daniel being there with him. The earl had set up his home, unpacked all his boxes, and the way everything had been displayed was just the way Victor would have wished, if he'd spared the time for the task. "I don't think so."

"Come on, you cannot spend every moment of the day here." Hambly glanced around. "It's not like you."

Victor faced the other man. "What I do with my day, both business or pleasure, is none of your concern."

The friendliness in Hambly's gaze dimmed. "Are you actually *mooning* over Lord Beecroft?"

He nodded. "I need to speak to him urgently."

Hambly shifted. "They say he's gone off and taken Marinari right from under Lord Bracknell's nose. The earl looked to be in a royal snit last night, let me tell you. He's impossible to speak with most times, but after recent events he's looking rather wild."

Victor agreed with Hambly's assessment of Bracknell's appearance. The man was clearly not happy and seemed to have no wish to speak to anyone but his father. "So I heard. I also heard his child has been unwell, which could account for his distraction. He's likely worried about his heir."

"A nurse will take care of the boy." Hambly shrugged, dismissing Victor's suggestion and continued, "Marinari has led us all a merry dance over the years. Mind you, we have that young thing, Felicity, booking rooms and such instead. She's become a favorite of many, so I doubt Marinari will be missed for long, mark my words."

Victor shifted in his chair. Marinari had teased many men in the club, but now he thought it over he couldn't ever remember her connected with a single man bar Bracknell. Daniel and Marinari had seemed friendly at most. Had Victor, and Lord Bracknell, mistaken affection for something more?

If Daniel was a spy, he should be quite capable of arranging an assignation with Marinari without anyone knowing. That they were supposedly found out seemed odd to him now. Victor didn't know whether to trust what he had seen anymore. Surely if they were engaged in affair, there could be no reason to leave the club. Marinari wasn't property. She was allowed to say no, and had done so on many occasions if the gossip was to be believed.

Uneasiness turned his stomach. What if it wasn't an affair at all? What if Daniel and Marinari's conversation had nothing at all to do with pleasure and everything to do with his work as a spy?

Daniel had said goodbye.

Guilt filled him immediately and he swallowed down his panic. Daniel had even warned him he wouldn't always be able to answer his questions. Victor stood, filled with tremendous agitation. What if it was all a distraction? His conversations with his competitors; the altercation over Marinari, leaving with Marinari and neither of them returning. Daniel could be risking his life at this very moment and Victor hadn't been willing to give him the benefit of the doubt. But how could he have known without some explanation?

He shook his head. The lack of sleep was making

him a victim of his own paranoia.

The dinner gong chimed through the Hunt Club suddenly and continued to ring much longer than normal. Victor frowned at the ruckus. He glanced at a nearby clock in confusion. "It's not the dinner hour." The chimes continued and the members around him climbed to their feet and turned for the dining room. Victor faced Hambly. "What's going on?"

"Have you never been here for one of Staine's impromptu meetings? So tedious. Last time some fool lost an item of value while dabbling with the whores again and we were all required to scour the club, chairs and to even turn out our pockets. I'm certain its nothing."

They followed everyone else into the dining room and found a place near a wall. Despite the time of day there were a greater number of members he'd not noticed come in. Was Daniel among them?

When he didn't find him, he focused on the Duke of Staines where he paced the flagstones before the fireplace. Nearby was Mr. Davis, his nephew Mr. Mumford and several of the members who had withdrawn funds from Victor's bank.

Victor glanced away. He didn't hold grudges, but he wasn't willing to forgive men who treated him unfairly. As the last stragglers hurried in, righting clothes and hair, Mr. Redding closed the doors and turned the key in the lock. He leaned close to Hambly. "This seems more serious than lost property."

Hambly remained silent and Victor glanced around the gathering. Mr. Mumford quickly averted his eyes when their gazes met again.

Staines set his hands to his hip. "My fellow members. The Hunt Club began twenty-odd years ago as a place where gentlemen may speak their minds with no repercussions beyond these doors. Unfortunately, it has come to my attention that not one but many gentlemen believe this rule does not apply to them and have spread gossip that has harmed another member's good standing in Society."

A rumble of disapproval swept through the dining room and Staines held his hands up for silence. "This gentleman has lost business unfairly, and although it is your right to change your mind about your affairs, an innocent man has been flayed by unsubstantiated gossip. It is a crime against our membership and our code."

Victor straightened his spine as Mr. Davis met his gaze. The man nodded definitively and Victor shrank against the wall. This meeting was about him and his recent troubles at the bank. *Dear God, the rumor had started here; among people I'd considered friends.*

"I tell you all now, with absolute certainty, those rumors are false and have been proven so by not one but three giants of industry. For your arrogance and unfair regard for the wellbeing of another member, the Club shall impose the highest penalties possible—a monetary fine and six month's banishment from the club's facilities." Staines drew a piece of paper from his breast pocket and called a roll. "Alexander, Hills, Forsythe, Leverett, Hollings, Marcourt, Fletcher. Those not in attendance have been written to this morning."

Some of the gentlemen were Victor's former clients. He glanced at Mr. Mumford as the man lean close to his uncle to speak into his ear. Why hadn't the banker's name been called? Hadn't he benefited from the gossip too?

Staines continued, "Gentlemen, please empty your pockets of all funds and hand the money to Mr. Redding."

A low murmur began among those seated as those shamed dipped their heads and their hands into pockets then moved toward Redding where he stood guard at the door. The clatter of coin into the receiving bowl grew loud and the room fell silent again until the collection was complete.

"Redding will escort you out in a moment, but I am concerned about the source of this vile rumor. I want to know who started it. I warn you that I do have some ideas of my own."

The group near the door stared at Victor.

"Mr. Knight," Staines called, "if you could step away from your current location I believe we can clear things up."

Victor moved and those assembled at the door continued to look to the place he'd been standing. But they hadn't been accusing him of starting the rumor. They were looking at Lord Hambly. Victor gasped as the shock hit him. He stared at Hambly. The man struggled to contain his emotions. "Why would you do such a thing?"

Hambly drew himself up straight. "So you would love me again."

"What?"

The members began to mutter amongst themselves and beneath the roar of sound, Victor's heart clattered painfully behind his ribs. Hambly had tried to ruin him. But why?

To hurt me was the only answer that came to mind. To take away something that mattered to him because he didn't like Victor's devotion to work. Because he was jealous of his success and of the time he willingly spent in his profession?

Victor drew close to him as anger filled him. "How dare you?"

"If you didn't work so hard you would have time for me," Marcus accused. "I loved you."

Daniel had been right. Revenge was indeed an ugly business. Victor had never once suspected Hambly could want to hurt him in such an underhanded way. "This isn't what you do for those you love. You make allowances for the things that matter to them."

I should have done the same for Daniel.

While he stared at Hambly, the Duke of Staines completed his sentencing. Hambly was to pay a thousand pound fine and endure banishment from the club for a year. That might not be long enough for Victor's comfort, but at least he'd be spared sight of the man when he dined at night.

Victor turned away and stalked to the end of the room. He stared out the window as his mind raced. He'd suspected Daniel of underhanded dealings simply because he'd spoken to Mr. Mumford. He put his head into his hands. The earl must think him a bloody fool.

A firm hand patted his shoulder and he spun around.

Mr. Davis smiled tightly. "The duke would like to speak with you to settle the debt."

Victor frowned and looked around the room. The dining room had cleared of most members and the doors were shut tight again. A bowl rested in the center of the table, coin and pound notes almost spilling from it. He didn't understand. "Your Grace?"

"Ugly business this." Staine's expression grew angry. "I take it you had no idea Hambly was behind the rumor?"

"None at all." Victor raked a hand through his hair. "I've lost quite a bit of business these past weeks, but I was baffled as to why."

The duke glanced at Mr. Davis. "Davis here pieced the puzzle together and came to me to stop it."

"My nephew actually asked about rule three a few weeks ago, and when I heard you were supposed to be in dire straights I came straight to you. You proved to me without a shadow of a doubt that it is not so." Davis smiled broadly. "I am glad to know your business is above board. I hadn't expected to have everything so plainly laid out and that spoke a great deal to me of your integrity."

Mr. Mumford approached next, his expression apologetic. "A few days ago Lord Hambly sought me out for investment advice. I was surprised but flattered and during the meeting he said something that alarmed me about you. He thought you'd be taking time away from your business affairs and suggested that mine would flourish as a result. He seemed strangely happy for me."

"Actually," Victor said slowly. "That is quite the opposite of what will happen. My business partner married a short while ago and his wife is expecting their first child. I expect to work even more hours than ever now."

"Oh," Mr. Mumford said wincing a little. "That will be hard. I run my concern alone and I'm overwhelmed most of the time. The demands of running a larger operation such as you have are undoubtedly more trying."

"I'll manage."

Staines gestured to the bowl. "The fines imposed on the members are yours to do with as you wish."

"I don't want their money," Victor protested.

"But it is yours by rights and you may disperse of it as you see fit. Give it away if you like."

Mr. Davis nodded decisively and exited the room.

His nephew began to follow, but Victor stopped him. "Mr. Mumford, may I ask you a question?"

"Yes, of course, sir." He nodded to the duke and they moved away from everyone else.

Victor hated to ask, but he needed to know about Daniel. "Might I inquire as to your last conversation with Lord Beecroft? It was here in the club I understand? What was it about?"

Mr. Mumford frowned. "We talked about my mother and how I can never make any sense of her accounts. I guess I disturbed him by groaning at their state out loud."

Well, that was a great deal more innocent than Hambly had suggested. "That's all?"

"Hmm, let me see." Mumford's eyebrows drew together. "I joined him because he invited me over to sit with him. He was alone. I worked. To be honest I don't remember much else but that he was kind and easy to talk to. I had an appointment next, though I doubt anything will come of that investment from Lord Hambly now."

Victor's eyes widened in shock. "Hambly really wanted to to invest with you?"

"That is what he hinted at, yes." Mumford shrugged, but it was clear he was disappointed to have lost the chance for new investment funds. "I'm sorry for what he tried to accomplish to your detriment. You've worked hard to get where you are and no one has the right take that success away from you. Certainly not in that manner." Mumford departed leaving Victor reeling yet again.

He had been so very, very wrong in his thoughts. Mr. Mumford was a very sincere young man. It was clear now that he'd picked up Victor's clients because they had *liked* him. He couldn't believe Hambly had so ably twisted everything about so thoroughly.

Staines moved toward him. "That man is quite the supporter."

"Mr. Davis?" Victor was very grateful for Mr. Davis' trust even more so now. "He's been with me since the beginning."

"Well, yes, Davis does speak highly of your expertise in financial fields, but I was referring to his nephew. Mr. Mumford holds you in the highest regard. I see a case of hero worship in the making if ever there was one." Staines patted his shoulder while Victor grew warm with embarrassment. "Decide what to do about the money soon. Redding will secure it in the house safe until tomorrow at the latest while you do."

Victor had no need of the money, but he nodded just so he could be alone with his thoughts. He really did owe Daniel that apology and fretted anew over what was keeping the earl away from London.

CHAPTER FOURTEEN

Daniel finished his report on the mission to the full committee of seven members to utter silence. "That is an end to it."

Lord Freeport's gaze bore holes into Daniel's head. "Are you certain?"

He had expected questions about The Angel's demise and had come prepared with all the answers he could give. "We were standing very close and although there was some cloud cover I am certain I hit my target and he either died immediately or drowned."

Freeport sat forward. "And if he did survive and swim to safety?"

Daniel would bet Freeport was regretting not asking to see the body now. "The Angel has a morbid fear of water, as you well know, my lord. He never got over the callous deaths of his grandmother and baby sisters." Daniel glanced at the other men gathered about the rickety table and noted their confusion. Clearly, as a group they didn't know *all* the details of The Angel's beginnings before he came into the King's service. "His family was weighted down and provided with just enough rope so they drowned in full view of land but had no hope of reaching for it. I recalled his fear of water last night and used it to my advantage. His escape was cut off in every direction. None of your men mentioned he surfaced?"

"No, they didn't."

Daniel surveyed his superiors, unconcerned they'd now question him about The Angel's death. If they'd asked to see the body, he might be in trouble. As it was they had to take his word, and the word of Freeport's best men, or call them all liars.

Several put their heads together in whispered discussion, so Daniel glanced about the room to give them privacy. This would be his last visit to this secret meeting place. It was so utterly boring that by next week, he doubted he would recall one aspect of the room.

When he faced his superiors again, the new gentleman promoted to replace Lord Pickens was watching him closely. Daniel didn't know Lord Warminster well except to nod at in Society, but he didn't need to better their acquaintance. "The Angel performed his last service for the Crown perfectly and you have put a stop to the leak created by the imposter Lord Pickens and Dominic Grendier. It is a shame to have lost The Angel's tracking expertise, but there you have it. I am quite sure you will replace him soon enough."

Lord Freeport nodded enthusiastically. "You shall have the best from our ranks with none of the added drama and of course our continued support in your endeavors."

Daniel smiled. "I gather you've forgotten the exact terms of my service to His Majesty. I brokered the deal that brought The Angel to this country and secured his services to deal with our little problems. However, with The Angel's death, my obligations have ended."

Lord Freeport spluttered, but Lord Warminster's gaze narrowed on him. "That is true, isn't it? Since my promotion, I've been going over past reports we have on you and you have our deepest thanks. I'd never have guessed you were more than you appeared."

Daniel wanted to bow extravagantly. Today was his finest performance as a spy, but he kept his reaction to a regal nod instead. "I shall not miss some of my duties, but it has been an honor to have served my King and country. I wish you good luck and good aim." He saluted them, spun on his heel and strolled out as if he hadn't a care in the world, aware that Lord Freeport was more than likely trying to work out how to drag him back into the King's service.

The man would not win in this round. He'd gotten The Angel's death and there was nothing left to bargain with.

He was free to speak his mind now. Free to share every facet of his day with the ones he cared for most.

His steps quickened as he rushed to hail a hack. He had two things to do before he ventured back into Society as an ordinary and dull gentleman of rank and wealth. He needed to speak to Lord Staines about The Angel's demise and hopefully make peace with Victor if it wasn't too late.

Victor was about to walk into dinner with Mr. Mumford and continue their partnership negotiations when a cry of anguish abruptly terminated caught his notice. Sounds of that nature were usually heard above stairs and not in the common rooms of the Hunt Club. He shrugged away his goose flesh and returned his attention to the business at hand. He was on the hunt for a new business partner. "What do think of our operation now you've had a better look?"

"I have to confess I am overwhelmed." Mumford rubbed a hand over his jaw. "How do you keep so many clients straight in your head?"

"Hawke and I keep our own clients files close but cross check each other's work. The clerks do the same. Hawke and I are very good at taking written notes during every interview. I highly recommend you do the same if that's not your common practice."

Mr. Mumford nodded. "Sometimes the conversation does get away from me and I don't do it until later."

"Then you would have a clerk take notes during the meeting on your behalf and afterward you would add your own notations if something were missed."

"I haven't staff yet."

"But at Hawke, Knight and Mumford, you would have several to assist you at all hours of the day. The clients you have would remain your own and any new clients will be divided between us as they come in. The clerks keep track, so it's all fair and equitable. Don't worry about the added burden. If the workload becomes unmanageable we'll simply hire more staff as needed."

"It seems a good arrangement."

Victor could see Mumford needed time and he wholeheartedly approved of his caution. It was a big step up for the young man, but if he joined their venture, Victor could imagine a bright future ahead for all concerned. "Don't rush to decide. There is ample time before I want to enforce my partner's reduced working hours. His wife is quite a darling and sets his mind at ease by visiting during the day. But in a short time she might become too large to make the trip easily. I do hope you like dogs. She has a small yappy ball of fluff that accompanies her quite often." A curse rang out and this time he couldn't help but glance around. "Did you hear that?"

"Hear what?"

"It's... would you excuse me a moment?" Since he appeared to be the only man to have heard the outburst, Victor hurried in that direction to investigate.

Ahead the office occupied by the Duke of Staines and his son for business matters loomed, the door slightly ajar. Inside, several men argued, but one voice stood out more than the others. He'd been hoping to hear Daniel's voice for more days than he'd care to think about.

Daniel's back.

Victor took a steadying breath and then approached the door. Through the gap he glimpsed Daniel resting against a desk and his heart clattered painfully.

The earl glanced up, but he didn't smile when their eyes met. He moved his head the tiniest amount, asking him not to come closer or speak. The man appeared utterly destroyed. While his appearance was impeccable, his eyes told Victor a great deal had changed. It was all his fault.

"He's dead. I was given no choice in the matter," Daniel said sadly.

Victor gasped in shock. Someone had died?

There was a long pause in conversation in the room and Victor tried to see to whom he was speaking.

"He's died before," the Duke of Staines spoke out in gruff protest.

Daniel shook his head. "You deserve the truth after all you've done for him. I am so sorry. Tell everyone

Marinari left for new employment, very far from here rather than the truth. It would not be in your interests for a connection to the two events to be made."

Victor jerked back against the wall just in time to miss being run down by Lord Bracknell as he stormed from the room. The earl practically sprinted from the club, his father and Redding hard on his heels.

Victor's head spun at the news. Victor peeked into the room. Daniel sat exactly where he'd been before. Relief brought a brief smile to his lips but his hear pounded as he advanced into the room. "Daniel?"

He studied Daniel carefully. He wasn't sure what to say next. He'd behaved so badly and now Daniel had lost someone he cared for.

Daniel stretched out a hand and Victor took it. "I missed you," he said simply.

"I missed you too, but—"

His lover pressed his fingers over Victor's lips before he could apologize. "I don't want to talk here."

"Very well," Victor said slowly. "Where then?"

The other man rose, drawing close. "Can we go home to your apartment?"

"Why not talk here?"

"Too many ears and too many tattletales willing to believe the worst of a man." Daniel's fingers tightened around his. "Will you take me home? I have so much I want to say to you."

Victor's heart skipped a beat. The man was clearly upset.

"Marinari?"

"Later, please." When Daniel offered his arm, he curled his around it. He would apologize soon, but he was too concerned over Daniel's distress to do more than agree to anything he wanted.

They slowly strolled to the front door in that fashion, releasing each other only when they took their hats and gloves. During the short ride to Victor's apartment, Daniel said not a word. He constantly turned his hat in his hands, proof he was as upset over Marinari's death as anyone, except perhaps Lord Bracknell.

Once in the privacy of his apartment, Daniel pulled him close. "Marinari had to appear to die by my hand or someone else would have been dispatched to do a proper job of it. I cannot allow anyone to believe he lives but I hope he does."

Victor stilled in his embrace overwhelmed by conflicting emotions. "Oh, my love."

Daniel crushed him, and pressed his face into Victor's neck. "I doubt I will ever know for sure if he lives, but I feel it to be so. He went under the water and didn't surface. I can only hope he remembered how to hold his breath long enough to save himself from drowning."

Victor ran his fingers through Daniel's hair. "Why are you telling me this?"

"I didn't want you to think I was capable of bringing harm to a friend." Daniel met his gaze. "Marinari was a work colleague to begin with and became a friend. Never, ever, more than that. Never the less, the loss of him from my life is a very real absence to me. I will miss him."

"I am so ashamed of my behavior." Victor drew back. "Him?"

"We have so much to talk about and we can now." The earl nodded then gently cupped Victor's face. "We hardly know each other and I've given you little knowledge of myself to expect your trust in everything. You were under a great deal of strain. I could see it. You had just as much reason to keep me in the dark about your problems as I did about mine."

"When did you suspect?"

"I was trained to be observant, to assess men's moods in an instant. My survival has often depended on quick thinking. That day I came to the bank, I saw you with your auditors, although I did not know what those men were at the time. It concerned me. That night you were very tense and when you asked about how to ruin a reputation the next morning, it wasn't hard to suspect all was not right for you."

Dear God had he been that transparent? "And you helped me?"

Daniel shook his head. "I had other business that took precedence. I would have wanted to help if I'd known and only if you'd asked me to."

He would never have asked but he appreciated knowing that he could have had help if he'd needed it from Daniel. "What really happened with Marinari?"

"One last assignment for the Crown. Well, two if you count his faked execution."

Victor's stomach lurched as the gravity and danger of Daniel's work dawned on him. "You place your self in danger by confiding in me."

"My service has ended." Daniel chuckled and swept his thumbs over the crest of Victor's cheeks. "Besides, it's not in your nature to divulge anything that might harm another. I know that about you very well."

Daniel was free to live as carefree a life as any gentleman of rank. That he'd returned to Victor at all was a miracle Victor wasn't sure he deserved. He cupped the man's face. "Thank you."

His lover kissed him softly. "I am sorry about what Lord Hambly did to you. Staines is livid and warned me not to place any faith in the lie circulating. I could see at once why he did it. He wanted you to need him more than anything else in the world."

"He didn't understand me." Victor caught Daniel's head against his. "Not like you do." He kissed Daniel fiercely, determined not to miss this second chance. The earl had to know he was wanted and desperately, but also that he was loved. Victor slid a hand beneath Daniel's jacket and waistcoat, holding the man tight against him. "How long can you stay?"

Daniel's face grew serious. "Forever, if you'll have me. I love you."

Victor removed his glasses, his heart bursting with excitement. "I love you with all my heart, so forever it will have to be."

EPILOGUE

The village was grey and dull and not the kind of place Daniel wished to stay in long. The mill in the distance was no bright feature on the horizon either. He strolled the short lane back and forth, stretching his legs after the long journey from London. Night was falling and according to the proprietor of the inn behind him his quarry was due to return soon. He strained his eyes and ears to catch sight of movement or sound on the road before him and detected nothing yet.

He was hoping to surprise Victor.

Again.

They had been lovers for six satisfying months and the man always appeared delighted to see him when he crashed these frequent investment trips of his. Daniel couldn't keep away from the man. He liked nothing better than to spend his nights in Victor's bed and their days in each other's company. Now that he was free to talk honestly about his life he held nothing back. Victor often accused him of babbling nonsense. Such teasing rebukes always were delivered with a lingering kiss.

No doubt he was becoming a pest and distraction but he had nothing else to do, in truth. His brother managed his estate just as well now as he'd always done. Quite frankly, he was sure his brother had been itching to kick him out last month when he'd made a short visit to the home of his childhood. So, he'd gone back to Victor's apartment and spent a pleasant week living with him and making love whenever the mood struck them both, which was often when his banker wasn't working.

Loving Victor was easy. Keeping up with him was much harder.

There was an energy about Victor that Daniel couldn't hope to match nor wish to change. Victor was always up to something. He had a very agile mind.

He jerked his head up as Victor's neat black carriage rounded the bend in the road. When he rolled past, face lit by carriage lantern, his head was buried in his papers and appeared completely unaware of Daniel's presence beside the road.

If Daniel didn't know Victor so well he might find that lack of recognition disappointing. Victor didn't mean to ignore him. He was simply terrible at juggling work and idleness, so he tended to work all the time.

He strolled up to the carriage doorway and opened it for his lover before the grooms could attend to it.

"Good, you're here at last," Victor said without preamble or showing any surprise to find Daniel in this remote village when he'd not been invited along in the first place. "I need your opinion."

"I'll assist if I can." Bemused, he followed Victor inside the Nags Head Inn and straight up the staircase to Victor's rented room.

Once inside the privacy of a bedchamber, Victor laid his papers across the table and slipped off his glasses to clean the lenses. "What do you make of that?"

Daniel approached the table and although he wasn't the least bit interested in meddling in financial affairs, he studied the flowing script. Victor was a prodigiously detailed note taker. If he didn't speak much he made up for it in his paperwork. After a moment of study, he set the papers down. "But this is mad."

"Good." Victor returned the glasses to the bridge of his nose. "I wanted a second opinion to be sure I wasn't losing my mind. The bank cannot invest in such an enterprise."

Daniel picked up the sheets again. "They give all the profit to the workers? Why drag you out here to see them if there's no profit to be had?"

"I've no idea. But I think the owner's completely lost his mind if he thinks we would give over our client's funds with no hope of a return. Coming here was a complete waste of time."

Daniel hated it when Victor was disappointed and moved to take his coat and loosen his neck cloth. To distract him even more, he brushed his fingers across

Victor's throat, noted his tan needed a few more hours in the sun to have a chance to be called such a thing. "I can make you feel better."

Victor smiled and caught his hand. "You always do. But this following me around simply cannot go on in its present form."

Daniel's heart sank. "I didn't think you were surprised enough."

His lover moved to cup his jaw. "How would you like to work for the bank, in an advisory capacity, of course?"

"Work?"

Victor shrugged. "You are at the bank almost every day, you sneakily follow me out of Town every time I investigate new investment opportunities or visit clients. You have helped grow Hawke, Knight & Mumford more times than you realize and you should really be compensated for your dedication. People will talk soon if I don't make you a part of the business anyway. I discussed the matter with my partners before I left London and they are in agreement. Plus, I think you could use an active occupation to fill your days."

Daniel regarded his lover steadily and then laughed. "I suppose I could learn to take your orders."

"Hawke's and Mumford's too. They each will want access to your expertise and company." Victor kissed the tip of his nose.

"I am in your way."

"Oh, no. But if we want to continue to avoid speculation and gossip about our close friendship then our arrangement needs to be seen as legitimate rather than intimate." Victor softly stroked Daniel's ear lobe and his cock swelled. "I do enjoy spending my days and my nights with you. I just want to make sure nothing can ever prevent that."

Daniel kissed Victor. They were lucky to have so much in common outside the bedchamber and they both knew it. Daniel's past made him suspicious of everyone and his own investigations had led to both investment and withdrawal of investment where a situation had changed in time to prevent any loss for the bank's clients. Working for the bank would make him a permanent part of Victor's life and that was all he needed for his own happiness. "I accept."

"Excellent. Since we've no room for a desk for you I don't imagine you'll mind sharing a corner of my office in the beginning?"

They could spend all day together, and the nights too. He worked hard to suppress a grin but ended up laughing anyway. "Sounds a very sensible decision to me, Mr. Knight."

"I do try to live up to your expectations."

"You always do." Daniel dug into his pocket and extracted the black box housing the gift he'd had made for Victor. "For you, my love."

Victor had not grown used to endearments or receiving compliments or surprise gifts and appeared startled. Daniel chuckled and opened the box to show him the signet ring he'd commissioned to be made. A gold band with a heavy, coin-sized circlet on the top, engraved with Victor's initials in the center and a discreet D and a W for Daniel Wellham engraved in tiny letters on the left and right. The casual observer would never notice he'd added his own name, but Victor certainly did.

His blue eyes grew glassy as he studied the piece. "I don't know what to say, but thank you. You are too good to me."

Daniel slipped the ring onto his finger then kissed it. He was so much in love with this man that he almost couldn't breathe for his joy.

Victor tugged Daniel to the bed and pushed him down onto his back. Then covered him with a soft groan. "I love you. So much I cannot describe it. It is beyond reason or value. You mean everything to me, but I have nothing to give you."

Daniel looped his arms about Victor's shoulders and smiled up at him. "You already have. Propositioning you, being a part of your life now, is the best thing I've ever done."

"That's not enough." Victor shifted and pressed a kiss beside his ear. "I've been so selfish."

He blinked at that pronouncement. "I don't see how."

"You once asked me if I liked to fuck men and I said not often. But I've never tried once since we've been together. You must have noticed my avoidance of it." Victor gnawed on his lower lip a while, making it very red when released. "I'd like to make love to you tonight the way you have to me all these months."

"What's brought on this nonsense?" Daniel cupped Victor's face. "I've never wished things were different in the bedroom between us. What we do together is incredible. Trust me. I love nothing more than to boss you around in bed. It excites you. It excites the hell out of me."

At his words, Victor's eyes flickered with uncertainty. "You're sure you don't think me less of a gentleman because I prefer to be tupped all the time?"

"Never." To prove his point, Daniel flipped them over and pinned Victor beneath him. He raised their arms to the mattress beside Victor's head, and by grinding his stiffening length against Victor's he eventually earned an excited gleam in his lover's eyes.

Making love once tonight would not be enough for either of them. It was funny how once never was. This love they shared had absolutely been worth the wait.

Daniel leaned close to Victor's ear and licked the lobe, before he whispered. "I'll be very happy to prove to my new employer just how dedicated I plan to be in making him deliriously happy to have me around. Starting now."

THE END

ABOUT THE AUTHOR

Determined to escape the Aussie sun on a scorching camping holiday, Heather picked up a pen and notebook from a corner store and started writing her very first novel—Chills. Years later, she is the author of over thirty romances and publisher of several anthologies too. Addicted to all things tech (never again will Heather write a novel longhand) and fascinated by English society of the early 1800's, Heather spends her days getting her characters in and out of trouble and into bed together (if they make it that far). She lives on the edge of beautiful Lake Macquarie, Australia with her trio of mischievous rogues (husband and two sons) along with one rescued cat whose only interest in her career is that it provides him with food on demand.

You can find details of her work at
www.heather-boyd.com